Pan's

Characters

Ekophoditus 'Eko', son of Madhavi & Philo

Jackie 'Jay', an Egyptologist

Jeuy, a diviner by dice

Madhavi, Philo's mistress and mother of Eko

Philo, Zenobia's husband

Zenobia, a woman of Roman Egypt

Pan's Road

By Mogg Morgan

Mandrake of Oxford

Copyright © 2006 Mandrake & Mogg Morgan

First paperback edition

All rights reserved. No part of this work may be reproduced or utilized in any form by any means electronic or mechanical, including *xerography, photocopying, microfilm*, and *recording,* or by any information storage system without permission in writing from the publishers.

Published by
Mandrake of Oxford
PO Box 250
OXFORD
OX1 1AP (UK)

A CIP catalogue record for this book is available from the British Library and the US Library of Congress.

186992889x

Contents

1	The Curse	7
2	Sickness	24
3	Zenobia's dilemma	29
4	Kasr el Einy	37
5	House of Life	48
6	Lost	63
7	Camels	72
8	On Pan's Road	76
9	Hephaestus' tale	85
10	Caesura	94
11	Kamsin	100
12	Rage in the desert	108
13	The Seven Caverns	120
14	The Hermit's Lair	131
15	On the road again	150
16	The Cobra's nest	159
17	Flight to the river	170
18	Ombos - Citadel of Seth	177
19	Head loss	185
20	The Bull of Ombos	193
	Glossary & Maps	221

Acknowledgements

To Robert Jackson,

author of *At Empire's Edge: Exploring Rome's Eastern Frontier*,

To Charlotte, for telling me to get on with it

To Kym, amanuensis and critic.

1 The Curse

'The desert is so vast it can only be painted in miniature'

Brion Gysin, *The Process*

Coptos is an ancient place full of hungry stones that soak up stories much as they once soaked up their inhabitant's blood. One stone in particular now absorbs hours of sweat from the gang of archaeologists toiling to loosen the hard earth from its edge. When it finally moves, there is hope that this nondescript block of sandstone will reveal hidden things.

Coptos, home of the temple of Isis & her ever-ready husband Min, had long ago been erazed from history by the brutally efficient Romans. You could count on the fingers of one hand the interesting inscriptions from the area. When Professor Sir William Matthew Flinders Petrie, archaeology's 'all father', first excavated, it was all he could do to trace the outline of one building, so thorough was the destruction!

The dark shadow of the stone was retreating. Slowly,

after nearly 2000 years, it exposed a cool socket of reddish-brown earth to the light of the sun. Moving between the workmen, Jay, the pit supervisor, squinted in the mid-morning sun, her eyes looking for any trace of decoration. There was none – it was yet another uninteresting piece of limestone pavement.

Or so she thought, until the 'Qufti' pointed with his crowbar and grunted. He was indicating a slight irregularity. At that very same moment, Jay spotted it too, the undoubted beginnings of a long, oblong shaft, skew to the wall of one of the chambers and running under it. The shaft was clogged with demolition rubble. The shaft held all the promise of a concealed tomb. But all the signs were that it had been disturbed and no doubt robbed out in Roman times, if not before. Even so, Jay set her most trusted workmen to the difficult task of removing the rubble, whilst she would exam the spoil heap for any objects the robbers had missed.

In the shaft were scattered two types of ushabtis, one of green glaze, another of clay painted yellow but not baked. These were of XXIInd dynasty style when Egypt was in serious decline. So too was the wooden head from a coffin lid, some small wax figures of the four genii, and fragments of red leather braces.

At the bottom of the shaft, 13 feet down, two small chambers were opened. These were cleared out and found to be empty. Lastly, the heap left in the middle of the shaft was removed, and in it, in a space about 2 feet square, was found a lead box about 18 x 12 x 12 inches. On the lid was roughly incised the figure of a dog, probably a jackal.

Jay's heart skipped a beat. Lead was almost universally the metal of death. The god Osiris was given a lead coffin by his murderous brother Seth. It turned out to be the ultimate ' gift horse'. Equiped with such a coffin, the immortality of Osiris was assured. So was Seth merely guilty of bad timing?

Many lead coffins, including some belonging to the Romans, had been found by archaeologists. These coffins, when cut down to more manageable strips, for use as a convenient curse tablet. Hence the trepidation about the contents of this tiny lead box. There was the strong possibility of a 'maleficarum', perhaps a body part, maybe a heart?

When Jay prized open the lid, the box turned out to be one third full of papyri in the final stages of disintegration. On one of the larger fragments, she saw characters of XIIIrd dynasty hieratic script. When she tried to lift this delicate fragment between her finger and thumb, it disappeared in a puff of 4000 year old dust.

Before this unfortunate accident, Jay read several words of the tantalizing document - 'bury her and inherit'. She knew the remainder of the papyrus was just too delicate to be unfolded, and would need to be packed with care, and sent straight to a conservation lab.

In the box remained a bundle of reed pens, 16 inches long and a tenth of an inch in diameter, and scattered round them were many small objects. Jay could see parts of four ivory wands, incised with the usual series of mythical creatures. A bronze uraeus entangled with a mass of hair. A crude doll, without arms or legs. An ape in blue glaze, an ivory Djed pillar and a coarse lotus cup in blue glaze. There was also a dancer's ivory casternet, its handles engraved with two lions. Scattered amongst all this were seeds, probably, so Jay thought, dom palm or balanites. Her hand fell next on a very curious ivory fragment of a boy with a calf upon his back. Other animals included a cat and an ape in green glaze, and a handful of beads. These were sometimes simple spheres of amethyst and agate; or barrel-shaped in haematite and carnelian; glazed and carnelian beads of the shape of an almonds, and one covered with minute crumbs of glaze. Jay's eye next fell on a green glaze object, the size and shape of a cucumber. Similar objects had been found all over Egypt although their function was still a mystery. 'You little beauty!', she said, her her hands cupping the wooden figure of a dancer; a masked girl, holding bronze serpents, one in each hand. Although the box's owner had long since disappeared, this could be only one thing. A magician's box, full of the tools of his, or her trade, plus a small library of their most treasured books!

Delighted with the finds, Jay was still a little puzzled as to why such a treasure trove should remain, when all the other chambers were completely robbed out. It was Joseph, the campaign leader who came up with a theory. The XIIIth dynasty interment was discovered and robbed long ago, perhaps by the workmen building a new tomb. The valuables being taken away and the other objects thrown out into the shaft and left. When the site was ruined and had been given over to some families of later times to use as a cemetery, the ready-made shaft was again utilised; it was cleared out until the mouths of the chamber were reached, and in them the second burials were placed. At some later period these too were disturbed, but in neither of the two last instances was the bottom of the shaft reached: so that when they, after finding the chambers empty, cleared completely the ground between them, they found this patch covered with the remains of the first interment. That was his theory anyway.

Over supper that night, Jay did her best to talk it down. But, as the effect of the duty-free loosened her tongue, she mentioned her theory, of a possible letter to the dead - a 'bury her and inherit.' This enigmatic phrase caught the attention of Joe, the campaign leader. Ancient Egyptian law allowed that whosoever paid for the funeral, might also inherit from the estate. A letter to the dead implied something had gone wrong. The deceased was being called upon for a remedy. Apart from her gender, the deceased identity was mystery, as so was that of her correspondent. This one, finding himself out of pocket, had resorted to magic.

Like all established academics, Joe was fond of teasing his subordinates, especially 'the ladies' as he called them. Egyptology, had its share of potentially embarassing subjects. There was fun to be had, leading the unwary student into a morass of double entendres, then watching them struggle to extricate themselves. Jay had seen it all before, saw it coming, but allowed it to happen just the same. Somehow, she thought, it might be best to allow Joe, to divert the conversation. He made a seamless transition from 'letters to the dead' to the mythology of the god Horus. His eyes sparkled as he quoted Seth's lacivious one liner to Horus - 'what a fine ass you have there.'

Jay yawned, and amid nervous laughter, excused herself and left. Her valediction mostly unacknowledged, Jay returned to her room. She was dying for a spliff, which she fully intended to enjoy, with a good book, before drifting off to sleep.

But she could not settle to it. Something was troubling her. She felt very disassociated in her simple, but cluttered, hostel room. At supper she'd eaten a great deal of an unusually succulent salad. The mounds of luscious, green, leaves of Cos were delicious, she just couldn't stop eating them.

Now, Jay threw herself on the bed, lying there for some minutes, unable to summon up the energy to do anything much at all. A smile crossed her face. She remembered the connection between the phallocratic god Min and the lettuce. Very fond of lettuce was Min, she thought to herself, as were all other gods with a heavy sexual load, so to speak. She smiled again. Yes like, Seth, he was very fond of lettuce. Isis used this fact, to tempt him into eating a bunch, into which Horus, had cum his load, or was it Seth's? Either way, it was a shameful thing, when the semen, unexpectedly called out from inside Seth's body - 'here I am'.

Horus had got one over on Seth, in more ways than one. The night before, Seth had had his wicked way with Horus 'What a fine ass you got!' Seth's dick never really got anywhere near the Horian ass. Isis had drilled him in a dirty trick. 'Let it rub between your thighs' she said, 'Seth, your brother, will never know the difference' she said, 'catch the semen in the palm of your hand. When Seth sleeps, bring me that seed.'

The sap that oozed from a freshly cut lettuce was suggestive enough, not only that, but it tasted of opium. They kept that secret didn't they, the bitter herb has long been bred out of the domestic variety, but now and again, the modern, cultivated, lettuce, remembers its seamy past. Jay was certainly getting a hit from something now.

She was possessed. By what exactly, well she couldn't say. Then the thought of something brought a sweet smile to her pretty face - 'the spirit of the supermarket' - that was it. If people could fall into trance at 'Bingo' or find ecstasy at a football match, then why not at the Middle Eastern cornucopeia - Zenobia? Yes Zenobia of Koptos!

The image of a woman's face erupted into her mind. It was a kind, open face. The owner was pretty, perhaps beautiful. Her long auburn hair, tightly plaited, parted in the middle, was dressed in the 'Isis' style, popular amongst wealthy matrons of Roman times. Her complexion was good. Her nose long and straight, rising to kind eyes and a thick dark brow that almost met in the middle of her forehead. Adorned in all of her finery, a gold band to hold her veil, gold earrings, necklace, rings. Her best dress, a bodice of good cotton dyed a venusian green, a coppery sleeve dress suspended from black shoulder straps edged with gold. In her right hand she clasped several lotus flowers, symbols of resurrection.

But she looked troubled. Jay spoke directly to the picture in the book that lay open on the bed: 'Something wrong is it?'

'Something bad is coming,' Zenobia sighed, 'and the end will be soon. We have all been living in a paradise for fools. The end is coming. I see it clearly.'

Jay wanted her imaginary informant to tell the whole story. 'You'd better start at the beginning,' she prompted, 'let me have it, your story, tell me your story.'

'My story! Do you have time for that,' Zenobia paused before continuing, warming to her subject, 'where do I start?'

'Well,' Jay replied helpfully, 'why not start at the beginning, why are you here, in this place?'

'Ah Koptos,' the name sighed from Zenobia's lips, 'I am here, because Philo, my husband, wants me here, wants me to stay in a house rented fom my cousin Pasos, the local papyrus merchant and bookseller. There is war. So now he and our adopted son Ekophoditus are trapped in Alexandria. Little does Philo know that I have been quite happy here without him. There' she said, making a large sweep with her arm 'I live just over there, past the Moon gate, behind the hot bathhouse, westwards, down some steps and up and after the precinct of the temple, to the right is a seven story house near the statue of Fortuna. I live opposite the shop of Jeuy, the diviner by dice. Juey, yes, he is my best friend in the city.'

She paused breathless, then continued, 'My husband thinks I am waiting patiently here until either he sends for me, or comes to bring me home. But the news from Alexandria is troubling. It is eleven years since the day emperor Diocletian began to rule us from Rome. Now he comes in person, together with his co-rulers, to supervise the reduction of a mighty city of a million souls. Alexandria and the blessed land that lies beyond. Word is that he has cut the aqueducts that convey the waters of the Nile into every quarter of the Alexandria. They say his camp outside the city walls is impregnable to the sallies of the besieged multitude, including my 'former' husband. When the legions of Diocletian do attack, it is always with caution and vigour. After a siege of eight months, Alexandria, wasted by the sword and by fire, now implores the conqueror for mercy, but Diocletian wishes the inhabitants to experience the full extent of his severity, as a lesson to others. Many thousands of the citizens have already perished. He has promised that very few will escape the promiscuous slaughter to come. He offers a barren choice - death or exile. He says when he does enter the city, the slaughter will not stop, not until his horse is wading knee deep in the blood of his enemies!'

Zenobia broke off, and with a habitual gesture, readjusted her fine cotton veil, drawing it close around her head. Wrapped in this veil, Jay could still see her face, her eyes moist but still twinkling wickedly, despite the sadness for the people of Alexandrian and for her own happy life that was about to change.

Jay did not know what to say, how should she comfort her? Jay knew the eventual outcome of the episode Zenobia was relating. And the knowledge of it momentarily sent her own gaze awkwardly to the floor. Jay looked up just in time to catch the faintest glimpse of Zenobia's elegant back, as she moved off through the moon gate, disappearing into the shadows. The vision ended.

Jay never got headaches. The next morning Jay woke with the most god-awful headache. Even with an iron will, it took her all morning to get going. She felt sick and so sensitive to the light, work was only possible, when wearing sunglasses. As the sun went down, several aspirins later, her stomach burning, she felt the pain begin to drain from her aching head.

A menstrual thing? Was she due? She ought to know, but she was a little out of touch with her body. Yes, she was due, maybe tomorrow.

Tomorrow came and went and still no show. It made her think. Had she had a period since returning from the visit to her friend Murugan in India?

'Oh no,' she thought, 'not again!'

A week slid past. Jay was again working late in her room. Her concentration waning, she was distracted by a sudden flashback to the week before. She felt the presence of

Zenobia, just behind her. Jay spoke first, without turning, just a whisper, 'Hello, it that you, Zenobia?'

She felt Zenobia's reply.

In the week since the first 'visitation' Jay made a point of reading a few things about the siege of Alexandria. Diocletian's bloodcurdling promise was, mercifully, never quite fulfilled. He did enter the city on his horse, but it slipped on cobbles, greasy with human blood. Diocletian was forced to dismount, as a small phalanx of the Praetorian Guard made a fierce protective ring to cover his back. When he looked at the knees of his horse, he saw they were smeared with blood. Diocletian, being ever mindful of the implied omen, thought then that the gods had decided the killing should stop. The killing stopped.

Many citizens survived the terrible siege. Enough to pay for a special equestrian statue, to commemorate Diocletian's fortuitous riding accident. 'Pompey's Pillar' is still there, in front of the remains of the Serapeum. Erected by Diocletian, to commemorate his victory over the usurper Domitius Domitianus. With these details still fresh in her mind, Jay asked whether there was any news of Alexandria?

'Alexandria,' Zenobia replied in a voice quivering on the verge of tears, 'I have heard nothing since the end of the siege, weeks ago. Why do you ask?'

Reality check, Jay thought to herself, *This is all a game. A game my mind is playing with itself.* The door-stop, rationality, firmly in place, Jay was silent for a moment, trying to untangle the small shift in time that seemed to exist between Zenobia's world, and her own.

She'd try an open question: 'Is there any news of your family?' her voice rising tentatively on the last syllable.

'No, nothing . . . but there is news of her!' She said, spitting the pronoun from her mouth.

Jay guessed the other woman, as in 'the other woman'. 'Oh,' she said, rather lamely, 'would you like to talk about it?' Part of her hoped not, Jay was not really a good listener.

But Zenobia was already speaking, 'My family,' she began, 'being well to do traders, did what all parents must do to make a good match for their firstborn daughter. I was comely enough and there were suitors aplenty. I was afterall very young, healthy of body and pleasing of face. But they figured to make for me a good match amongst the sons of another guild family. And so it was that I was betrothed to Philo.'

The corners of Zenobia's mouth curled ever so slightly, as if tickled by Philo's name. She went on: 'I could not believe my luck, for he was not a great deal older than I, elegantly handsome and seeming in everyway a good man, destined to make a success of life.

I knew that Philo, their choice, like all men, must have his faults, but I did not really care, not then.' Zenobia's smile had evaporated.

'Soon after our wedding night, he told me, though he would try his best to be a dutiful husband, he was not sure if he would be able to fulfil, all of the many expectations, I might have of him. This he would do out of respect for both our families. My dowry was not large, 10,000 silver drachmas, six pairs of gold earrings, a fine gold crescent, six gold rings, a pair of silver armlets, two bracelets, a box of robes, ten mantles, copper vessels and a basin, 1000 minae of tin and thirty and three quarter arourae of land, this land to revert to my father if we divorced.

Turns out he had married me out of obligation to his father, although in truth, men do not worry too much about their father. In our lands it is the daughter who must go out and support their parents. Philo would be free, as he had always been free, to have a fine life with or without me. Even so, he hoped I was able to overlook certain faults in his character. Naturally I asked him what these faults might be, to which he replied three; a love of women, an addiction to gambling and a dalliance with politics. He was a courtier to Domitius Domitianus, the one called the usurper by Diocletian.'

Jay was beginning to get a firm impression of Zenobia's

character. She had not said which of the three faults, would to her, be the most distressing; a promiscuous husband or the dangerous political friends? She was hardly the type one would describe as of few words. Jay tentatively asked, whether Philo was currently having an affair. To this, Zenobia, obviously lying, snapped 'he was not'.

After a moment's thought, Zenobia completely retracted what she had just said, totally contradicting herself. Her husband, had indeed become infatuated, with a hetaerae, known as Madhavi. Goodness knows how she came to be in Alexandria. 'She was an *indu*, a worshipper of Maia, as Isis is known in their lands. And much as it twists my stomach to admit it, a renowned beauty, a dancer, with a fine singing voice, able to accompanying herself on the lyre.

She could have had her pick of any number of men that swarmed around her, like flies on a dung heap. But my husband Philo, being so besotted, ignoring my own blandishments, had wagered that he would be her favourite, and somehow, he won his bet, when he promised to lay at her feet, her entire weight in gold, if she would be his.'

'There was the root of it.' Zenobia continued, obviously warming to her topic, ' If he had left me, to live with her, then maybe things would have been for the best. But when he married me he was already in love with another woman. Philo wanted my dowry, in effect he had pledged my wealth, for the lifestyle of Madhavi, with whom he had secretly set up a second house. Whether I liked this or no, I paid for it, one way or another.'

The conversation dried up. But before Jay could open her mouth, Zenobia continued saying 'many years have passed since our wedding. When my mother was on her death bed, looking forward to meeting again with my father on the otherside, she told me her only regret was that Zenobia had not given her any grandchildren.

I didn't really have the heart to tell her the truth. And as it happened it was not for want of trying. Philo was, is, a very considerate man. Despite his nights of passion elswhere, there was always something left for me.

A guilty look passed over Zenobia's face. Besides, a woman has her own needs. I learned from a priest in the temple of Min, the god of male generative power, how a regular diet of Min's vegetable, the moist lettuce, would keep a man in good condition, in that department. When Philo made his regular visit to our home, I made a point of always preparing delicious, aphrodisiac salads. This way I hoped I might one day make him forget Madhavi. What a young fool I was. But I never did become pregnant.' Zenobia said, biting off the words, unable to hide her frustration. She lowered her gaze, as if in shame, 'but *she did.*'

Why, Jay wondered, was this obviously intelligent woman

waiting for news of a man, who had squandered her money, set up home with another woman of dubious reputation, and fathered a bastard? Jay abandoned this thought, just in time to see Zenobia, disappearing into the twilight.

Jay decided it was time to write to her friend and sometime lover, Murugan. She wanted to tell him she might be pregnant.

2   Sickness

An unfinished letter waited in its envelope for Jay to find a convenient time to put it in the post. She unfolded the neatly typed, single sheet and, in an unused corner, wrote a brief paragraph, concerning her current predicament:

> PS: Strange things are happening to me at the moment - in more ways than one. Makes me think I might be pregnant - JUST JOKING! It started as a sickly headache. I woke up most days to this and it took the rest of the day to throw it off. My breasts were aching and my nipples very tender. I need to get checked ou by the quack. I thought we must have been careless or something, during my last visit. Us,

```
careless!! I started thinking,
second time lucky, although really
you know how I feel about these
things, It's probably some kind of
hormonal problem. It's damned
inconvenient! But don't worry
overmuch - it's being sorted, I'll
keep you posted if there are any
unforeseen developments. You are
the nearest thing I have to family.
Think of me. J
```

Jay quickly scanned the rest of the letter: 'I find myself at the beginning of a new enterprise, in more ways than one. I'm still at Kom el-Momanien, just outside Qift, on the Nile, the place known in Greek as Koptos but by the natives as Gebtu. Even considering how old this place is, it's pretty difficult to find two stones lying on top of one another; at least no two stones from before the coming of the Romans. It was the Romans, surprise, surprise, who destroyed everything that came before, rebuilding only some of their own temples, with the stones of other, ancient buildings. When Flinders Petrie (Victorian 'Old Git'), excavated the meagre remains, in the late nineteenth century, he found some very, very old sculpture, reused as the foundations of a Roman temple. These turned out to be the oldest religious images anyone has ever found here. If you ever come to visit me in Oxford, I'll take you to see them, these colossal white-stone images are of a god known as Min. The relevance of this will soon become clear.'

Jay refolded the letter, replacing it in the envelope. She made a mental note, to post it the very next day. She had lots to do; see the doctor, put things in hand. But again the headache; a real stinker. Looking down at the unmade bed, her eyes were greeted by an even more worrying sign. The indentation left by her head on the pillow, was a nest of fine blond hair. Panic. Was she loosing her hair? Alopecia is scourge of female academics. A kind of 'I told you so', from the predominantly male establishment. The wagging finger that said, 'you see - this is what happens when you try to be like men'.

They weren't really friends – you didn't have friends among other academics – there was just too much competition. You can't be friends with someone, who's going to look over your shoulder, passing off what they see as their own work.

More hair fell in the shower. She dried herself off and phoned the local doctor retained by the British School of Archaeology. He took the call. In a babbling burst of data, she told him her fears and symptoms.

He wasn't too sure what to think. Maybe she should go straight to a specialist in Cairo? He could arrange it. In the meantime he prescribed some good painkillers, to deal with the headaches. Jay should see his nurse, for a discreet pregnancy test. An appointment was made with a specialist at the Kasr el Einy hospital, in Cairo.

A few days later, a letter arrived from the hospital. The letter gave Jay that sinking feeling. It said that the specialist had looked at her case. To save time, he suggested a stay of one week in the hospital. This would allow him to do a whole load of tests; these were best supervised in a hospital environment. 'A week in hospital, that's his idea of saving time!' Jay wondered whether 'in order to save time', she might as well pack up and head back to Oxford. But that meant leaving the dig early. She looked at the appointment - first week of October 1981.

Jay wondered if she was becoming too butch? Surrounded mostly by male colleagues, the best she might expect was the advice that, loosing your hair was natural as one got older! Had they even noticed she was a woman? Jay had forgotten she was vain. She was a tomboy; clothes strictly utilitarian. Was she a real woman? Why me, she thought, why does it have to be some woman's thing? Jay ploughed on with her work as best she could, saying nothing much to anybody. She would have to find an excuse to be away for a week in Cairo. No problem. Her colleagues would probably be happy to see her gone. It gave them chance to rifle through her papers; see what she was really up to. Jay wished she could phone Murugan. At least she could talk to him. Too much hassle, too much hassle. Returning to work, she found the days dragged. Archaeology, that had once seemed so interesting, had become drudgery. Her only relief, the thought of day's end at two. She longed for the evenings, to be alone. Perhaps her imaginary friend, Zenobia would come. Jay could talk to her, couldn't she? Zenobia was a sister, Jay could tell her anything and everything.

3 Zenobia's dilemma

Jay waited patiently on her bed, anticipating Zenobia's quiet approach to her room. It had become a nightly ritual. Sometimes it happened twice a day, first during the afternoon siesta, then again, later, in the evening. One such night, Zenobia came, clutching to her bosom, a small piece of papyrus – a letter. Unprompted, she began reading the contents. 'It is from Madhavi', Zenobia began, smugly 'she says I am a good woman, but how can she know that, we have never met? But then she says she has met me, that she has heard me sing in the Iseum.'

'The Iseum in which you were a singer?'

'Yes indeed,' Zenobia replied, 'for many years I have done so. It is a tradition among the women of my family. I know all the songs of course, the whole story. Zenobia took a quick breath and began to sing:

> Beautiful Youth,
> Beautiful Youth
> Come, come to your house;
> Beautiful Youth,
> Beautiful Youth
> Come, come to your house;
>
> Holy image of the earth,
> Essence of our time
>
> Beautiful Youth,
> Beautiful Youth
> Come, come to your house;

Jay recognised it immediately as 'The Lamentations of Isis & Nephthys,'

'Ah, I know that', she said. 'So you were Isis?'

'No', Zenobia replied in mock surprise, 'I took the lesser role, that of Nephthys.

In a voice less sweet, Zenobia began, with some power, to declaim a line, with all the stentorian tone she could muster:

> 'Be not unaware of me O Seth
> If you know me then I shall know you!'

Zenobia's voice changed subtly as she spoke. It was as if some unseen hand took her at the throat, squeezing her vocal chords, so her voice now reminded Jay of someone she knew, although for the moment she couldn't quite say who. It was a very odd transformation:

'Be not unaware of me O Nephthys
If you know me then I shall know you!'

The momentary illusion evaporated. Zenobia's voice again, this time reciting with obvious emotion, lines from the ancient verse drama:

'Wandering amongst the fields of rushes
I searched for the corn king
and there found him
sinking beneath the water
where his brother Seth had left him,
when his jealous rage had gone
I raised him up as Osiris and he spoke thus:
The reed boats are set down for me
that I may cross on them to the horizon
The nurse canal is opened
and the winding waterway is flooded
the field of rushes filled with water
and I am ferried over them to the eastern side of the sky
to the place where the gods fashioned me
and where I was born, new and young

> *convey to Horus the Eye that by its power*
> *This waterway may now be opened'*

Then, again the lector's voice, subtly modulating, becoming more masculine, resembling, in the mind of the listener, the essence of a man, a special type of man. Jay struggled to place it, this mercurial voice, like that of her closest friend, Murugan, secreted away in his South Indian retreat. It was not his voice, but it shared some of its timbre.

> 'Behold I can endure and stand no more
> Against Osiris who was nobler than I
> Your brother Seth will chill your heart no more.
> Oh my mother Nuit, stretch yourself over him
> And place him in the imperishable stars
> *which are in thee, so that he may not die.*
> Isis, utter the word and make it so
> let Horus possess the Eye!
> That I tore from him in our fight
> Horus the son shall in his father's place arise
> The prince shall now become the king.'

Now came a whole chorus of voices, melding with Zenobia's. Perhaps this was her special gift that so entranced Madhavi, secretly eavesdropping. When Zenobia sung, she was never unaccompanied:

> 'Fish of the deep, fowl of the skies
> Go seek Osiris where he lies!'

Silence fell. Then Nephthys again took up the theme:

> 'With my sister Isis
> widows of the corn king
> Have made him anew
> In the form of the Ankh
> symbol of eternal life
> Seth, as an oxen
> shall raise him up
> upon his back
> then remembering
> their quarrel
> throw him down again
> cutting him into fourteen pieces
> like the moon
> and the companions of Seth
> will eat of the bread of life
> How noble, fair and beautiful he is
> Seth struggles no longer'

Again, the voices of a chorus. The pace quickens:

> 'But there is a price to pay for such a sacrifice!
> Horus, the seed shall become the plant
> as the son succeeds the father,
> and receives the Eye of Power!
> Behold confederates of Seth
> *I will strike you as you struck my father!*
> I command you: thrash him no more!'

. . . the chorus really lets rip:

'Now in the fight
Horus tears the thighbone from you - Seth
He flings it into the sky, as a permanent memorial'

'Now in the fight
Horus tears the thighbone from you - Seth
and makes of it a plough
to scrap the earth
and plant the seed of his father
and as a mummy cloth is bound around a corpse
so shall our enermies be bound'

'And I, Great Nephthys, reunite his limbs!
And as a panther-cat destroy all evil.'

'Now in the fight
Horus tears the thighbone from you - Seth
and opens his father's mouth
so he may speak truly
Lord of the Upper and Lower worlds.

Now in the fight
Horus tears the testicles from you - Seth!
And grafts them to his own body
Thereby increase still more his potency!

The oil of my eye that gleams so brightly against Seth

Now raise ye up my father who lies here!
We are all embalmers
masked, our faces those of wolves or monkies
Our heads anointed with oil
we stoop and are bowed beneath the weight of him!
Now Nuit, raise us to heaven, for your back
A ladder is,
its vertibra the rungs.
My sister Isis
sing with me a final lamentation

Beautiful Youth,
Beautiful Youth
come, come to your house;
Beautiful Youth,
Beautiful Youth
come, come to your house.

Holy image of the earth,
essence of our time

Beautiful Youth,
Beautiful Youth
come, come to your house.

The last words faded into the dreamy night. Jay roused herself. She remembered Madhavi's letter. But Zenobia had gone, drawing her black veil around herself and walking quietly into the gloom. Jay opened her mouth, meaning to call for her to come back, come back. But it was too late.

Zenobia had gone. Jay must rest. She was elated. *Please*, she said to herself, *come again tomorrow night!*

4   Kasr el Einy

The snap of paper. Half a mile away the Muezzin had just opened his prayer-book. The microphone captured it all, as it did every morning - the hasty clearing of the throat, the intake of breath, the first bellowed notes of the call to prayer. In this part of town there was no need for an alarm-clock.

On the pillow, a demoralizing number of Jay's long fair hairs. She picked them up, everyone, wrapping them in a tissue, before dropping them into the bin next to toilet pan.

Six am. The early morning air already stifling. Jay grabbed her clothes, but felt uncomfortable in her habitual jeans and shirt. Suddenly it was all so constricting. She changed. This time more carefully into a loose fitting shalwar. The prayers had finished. She lay back on the bed, meaning to close her eyes, *just for a moment*, to let the painkillers kick in.

She opened them. It was ten-thirty. She was late, the day almost half over. On the phone to Joe, the big american campaign leader. She wasn't feeling too well. *Could she work in her room for the morning, come in before the evening lock down?*

'No need for that,' Joe replied, assuming his pastoral voice, 'They'd all gotten themselves invited to a special supper at the home of the local EAO inspector.' Unusually for the service, he wasn't housed with the dig, but actually lived nearby in Qift. In a reversal of the normal protocol, the inspector was going to feed them! And what's more, this one was actually interested in archaeology. He'd already intimated that he had questions for Joe, who was an expert in many fields.

'Which means', Joe said, 'he will have something for us to look at, something either the guy's collected or exhumed from his own garden. He'll be wanting to show them off. Probably not that exciting a prospect, but it's a nice gesture.'

Joe was to be a paragon of tact and politeness. He'd do his damnedest not to disappoint the guy. Everyone wants their little piece of Pharaonic history but weren't always happy when the stuff turned out to be Roman or Arab. 'But you know', Joe sighed, 'it's gotta be better than sweating the night out in the tent'.

Jay listened to all this, wondering what Joe would do if the guy showed him something really valuable. The Inspector would be quite well to do. After the 'business', he would call in some local entertainers, snake charmers most likely.

'Seen that a thousand times', was Joe's final valedictory. But you be sure and take care of yourself. Get yourself fit, take a few days off, come in when you want.'

Jay saw her opportunity to broach the difficult matter of time off. 'Funny you should say that. I was meaning to talk to you about that. I might have to take more than a few days off. The doctor says I need to go to Cairo for tests. It might be more like a week. Not straight away, maybe the week after next?? Not sure yet.

'That's OK', Joe crooned, 'take what you need'.

Jay put the phone down and wondered why he was being so nice.

* * *

A lonely private room in a Cairo hospital. Dr Habibi was the urological registra, turned out to be a she. Her perfect English had a slight American drawl, that spoke of study at an American college, probably, so Jay told herself, sabbaticals spent in the top US hospitals. Dr Habibi suspected some kind of pituitary disorder, but would need to work up a whole array of tests to eliminate any other endocrine involvement. That first day a large black and white tablet every two hours.

Outside the hospital such drugs would be so expensive, here the company would pay for all clinical trials. But there might be side effects, drowsiness; hence observation on a hospital ward was obligatory.

Jay was confused already. The events of the day merging one into another. The conversation with Dr Habibi was already a memory. It seemed so long ago, but actually it was just that morning.

Maybe it was the experimental drugs she'd prescribed, already coursing through her veins. Medicalization, that's what it was, Jay, pleased with herself to have remembered such a complex word. Medicalization, I'm medicalised, she said to herself. The whole process turned her brain to wispy shreds of lint. The monotonous quiet of a evening after a ridiculously early supper. The far away noisy streets, the all-pervasive hum of the city's evening traffic. The boredom, that had her staring at the Arabic calligraphy of the ward signs. Her eyes defocused as one Arabic letter morphed into another.

She could't say exactly when Zenobia arrived. First the voice emanating from an unseen radio. The power surged, swelling the volume. Moments later the lights went out - a power cut - business as usual.

'. . .I do not remember ever seeing Madhavi. She must have been disguised.' There was laughter in Zenobia's voice.

What was she talking about? Ah yes, her love rival Madhavi, who has been secretly observing Zenobia at the Iseum. Guiltily mingling her voice with Zenobia's in the song.

'Lustful woman,' Zenobia cursed, 'and not even circumcised!'

'Are you circumcised?' Jay thought.

'No' Zenobia replied smiling, 'but I do not need that to control my desires. She wants something, of course she does. She is trapped in Alexandria. She will not leave without Philo. My husband is one of the leaders of the rebellious city council; he will not leave while what he calls his 'people', are besieged. "Great food shortages", she writes, "things falling apart, of terrible things – people have eaten all animals in the city, and they say the Christians subterranean feasts have never been more popular". Isis preserve us from the cannibalism of our ancestors! she prayed.'

'What does Madhavi want?' Jay mumbled

Zenobia ignored the question. She preferred another. 'I am one of the two temple singers that serve the many Iseums of Alexandria and now Koptos.' Zenobia began to sing: 'Beautiful youth . . .'

'Zenobia!' Jay exasperated, had to interrupt, 'what does Madhavi want?'

Zenobia stopped her singing. 'She has sent a warning. One of her 'clients' is a 'master of secrets', a prophet even. The man has every reason to hate the Romans. Diocletian is convinced all these rebellions are financed by the secret Egyptian art, the making of gold. He hates all alchemists, and plans to burn their secret books, along with the owners. This man Heri, received a warning from his spirit guides. If Alexandria falls, Koptos will be next. Madhavi wants to send her child to me for safe keeping in Koptos, if all goes well, he will return to her when Alexandria is again safe. But, she says, if Alexandria should fall, I should, for my own safety, leave Koptos, before the Romans come. A blow in Alexandria, will be received threefold in Koptos.'

'Where does she think you can go?'

Zenobia again fiddled with her veil, then perched on the end of the bed, as if seeing Jay for the first time. She turned toward her with her kind expression on her face, saying quietly: 'you are sick.'

'Never mind that,' Jay responded, 'tell me where you will go?'

'Only if telling you is alright, if it will not distress you?'

'Yes, that's fine,' Jay snapped, struggling to suppress her impatience. Zenobia took a breath and continued:

'Madhavi knows I come from a trader family. She is no doubt thinking, that the Romans will not be able to recapture control of Pan's Road across the desert to Berenice. At least not until Koptos is in their hands. She is right. The Romans fear the Blemmyres, those who control the trade routes all the way to the sea. Madhavi knows I can easily escape to one of the ports on the Red Sea coast. In return for this warning, she wants me to take her child. If all is lost, I am to see he gets to Musiris in India, where Madhavi has family who will take him. . . '

Jay wondered whether Zenobia was capable of such altruism. The radio was fading. Suddenly she was so tired, the words tumbled in her mouth.

'I cannot decide what to do, I will ask Jeuy the diviner to cast for me . . .'

Zenobia faded into the shadows between a scratched oxygen bottle and the striped cotton curtain. Jay, light-headed from her medication, felt herself tagging along.

'Two thoughts were so mixed up I could not tell.'

The line of a poem on repeat. Was she Zenobia now? Instinctively she found Jeuy the diviner's rough little shop. His was a Jewish name. Boyish, some would say effete, in a way only a Greek could be. He spoke with an obscure and exotic accent. If Jeuy was a Greek, his blood must be mixed with that of another race. His ochre red hair was cut short and plaited closely to his scalp. His skin was dark, perhaps a trace of Nubian or Beja blood.

The Romans told many lurid tales of the Beja. Those desert warriors were not uncivilized, despite what th Roman's say. That old fool Pliny had called them the 'headless' ones. But Jeuy's head was very firmly on his shoulders. The garbled account of their appearance, was testament to the extreme antiquity of his race. Those very old legends that describe archaic burials; the corpse decapitated, to encourage the vultures to eat.

The Beja were worshippers of the god Seth, whose ancestral lands were very close to Koptos. Zenobia's family often dealt with the Beja. They filled a vacuum left by a shrinking Roman empire. The Beja maintained and controlled all the desert roads in this part of the world. Jeuy was 'in between' in more ways than one. His large, but elegant hands, smoothed a piece of fine linen over a rough table. She was fascinated and repelled by his long finger nails, long even for a woman. The shells were unnaturally white from regular cleaning.

Jeuy the diviner took a small papyrus roll from its hiding place, and lay it down gently on the cloth. With his delicate fingers, he deftly worked through the folios of the book. A single column of papyrus soon became two, as the prelims slid through the diviner's nimble fingers. The book, now fully unrolled, was weighted down with two small metal tokens. Jay's attention was drawn to the statuettes; they were lead.

Juey placed three, well-worn knucklebone dice, on the cloth. Under his breath he whispered a short prayer to his genii. A moment passed. With a nod, he indicated his readiness for the first question. Jay's hand shot out and took the dice, focussing on the question, as the first dice fell from her, or was it Zenobia's hand?

A three, followed by a four, then a two.

Before each little passage of the oracle, three columns were drawn in red ink. Even upside down, Jay could see they were numbers – Gamma, Delta, Beta.

The diviner's fingers flashed down the vertical columns to the corresponding passage: In curious, mangled vowels he told her: 'Act in what way your mind is moved, hold back no longer.'

'Umm' she felt herself thinking, 'if he thinks my mind is desperate to look after the child of another, then he knows me not.'

The diviner sensed her disappointment. Too vague. 'Always same, Zenobia, trader's daughter, cast again.'

Digamma, Beta, Gamma - 623.

Again the diviner's finger's worked down the columns. A smile grew across his face, then, at the realisation of something else, he blenched.'

'What does it say?'

'The great sea's expanse they across, this is the Earthshaker's gift to them!'

'Oh' she said, 'then we shall cross the great sea. The "Earthshaker" – the great god of the sea, Poseidon is it not?'

The diviner removed the die and rolled up his precious book. The "Earthshaker" is Neptune, yes. But I think it also mean the monstrous emperor, Diocletian.'

The diviner fell into thoughtful silence. Zenobia felt sure there was more, Juey was holding something back. 'Are you sure there is nothing else?' Zenobia queried.

'Yes, I think so,' the diviner replied, 'if you call in your mind the story of the "Earthshaker", you will understand the many hazards await you, on your journey. Odysseus, he take ten years to find his way back from home. Many times he was obstructed by savages. There are many savages on the Red Sea coast. Many are the strange tales I hear, better than Homer.'

'Is there a way out?'

'Yes, but you must take great care, you must not repeat Odysseus' mistake, offer insult to injury. Blinding Poseidon's son Polyphemos was necessary to escape the cooking pot. But deriding the god's child, that was too much. That long, perilous journey over water, was a punishment, sent by the gods. The oracle is clear, the despot comes, before you a perilous journey over water. There is much to beset you before you find safe harbour.'

Zenobia gathered her things ready to depart. Leaving another small obol coin, for the diviner's time. But before she could go, Jeuy gently laid his fingers on her forearm. It was a very familiar gesture, his hand resting there. 'Zenobia,' he said, 'take me with you. Two together would be easy. Surely you see the truth of that?'

'Yes', she replied, 'it might well be so. But I need to sleep on it, to think it through. She would sleep upon it. Let me give your answer on the new day.'

Jeuy seemed content. He moved aside so Zenobia (and I) could leave the shop.

5 House of Life

Hours sped by. For many of them, Jay remained trapped in the mysterious vision of Zenobia's life. Walking with her to her house, going with her about her business. It was not until she lay down to sleep, that Zenobia's bed became Jay's bed, and she was again in a Cairo hospital.

She was delirious. The night nurse was speaking so gently, Jay could barely hear her above the murmur of the sleeping ward. 'There was a call for you.'

She checked Jay's body signs, then held out her medication. Jay staggered to the lavatory, supported on arms, surprisingly strong. There she added another increment of urine to the plastic container that bore her name. Then back to the bed and the oblivion of a few hours sleep.

It was not the morning bustle of the wards that woke her,

but dawn over the ancient city of Koptos. The nurse had become Zenobia. 'wake up' she barked, 'and accompany me to the Hewet Neteru, the House of the Gods.'

The House of the Gods was the double temple of Pan and Isis, 'great of magic', his consort in these parts.

Time has passed. The dusty streets of Koptos seemed strangely melancholy. A palpable sense of dread formed the backcloth of Zenobia's thoughts. The rebellion in Alexandria, that had so swollen everyone's heart with hope, had failed. As Diocletian was in control of the city, fulfilling his blood thirsty vow. The genii of Alexandria had managed their final trick, causing the emperor's horse to stumble on the greasy cobbles of the Sun Gate at the entrance to Via Canopus. Good fortune for some is a bane for others. Madhavi's son Eko, had been secreted out of the city, and was at this moment safe in Zenobia's house. It was best not to dwell on the fate of his stranded family.

Koptos was full of talk of rebellion. The merchant king Firmus had briefly seized control of the town council, calling himself the new pharaoh. But when word came that Diocletian was sending one of his best, and most brutal generals to quell the trouble, the rebellion evaporated.

The talk was - if the slaughter at Alexandria was extreme, how much more so will it be for us? Agents provocateurs were everywhere, spreading disquiet and stories of how not one single stone would be left standing on another, by the time the Roman cohorts have done their cruel work.

Zenobia's plans of escape were well advanced. She needed to visit the great temple, whose gleaming new stonework, belied a structure older than time itself. She prayed to the great mother, prayed that they escape before the hammer descended.

Arrangements were in hand to move that very night. Zenobia would be the last of her people to move - the rest had already relocated lock, stock and barrel, before, as they say, the other shoe fell.

All the more important, this final visit to the temple of Min, or as the Greeks call him, Pan, guide of travellers in the desert, and Isis, protector of all mariners, and those who travel the high seas.

* * *

Zenobia woke when the eastern sky was still a predawn purple. She greeted the final few stars rising in the east with the sun god Ra:

'Hail, Ra in your rising,' she smiled as she whispered the words from the 'Book of Coming Forth by Day'. She roused her remaining servant to sort out the most recent arrival, the

PAN'S ROAD

young boy child Eko. Soon even that retainer would flee to relatives across the river. Zenobia busied herself with her own toilet, cleaning her face, rubbing her newly washed body with olive oil, repairing the dark kohl that would protect her eyes from the sun's glare and without which she did not feel complete.

She guessed that her friend Jeuy was already waiting patiently outside her locked door. They all three would take road to the northern gateway, where, outside the high city walls, was the ancient triple shrine of, Isis, Min and Horus the child.

Three together they went, through the already crowded western pylon gate and into temple's temenos. Zenobia bade them leave her, she had her own business in the Isis shrine. Jeuy was to guide Eko to the Horus shrine, assisting him to hand a small offering to the child Horus. They had their instructions to move quickly to the most southerly and ancient part of the sanctuary; the shrine of Min. They were to make offerings for safe passage along Pan's Road.

On the previous day, Zenobia had done her best to explained to Eko, how Pan was just another, more modern name, for Min. 'Min is everything,' she had told him, 'This temple may look new, but it is built on very ancient foundations. Some say they were laid at the beginning of the second creation.'

Eko interrupted her: 'second creation, when was the first?'

'Ah' she said, brushing the question aside, 'that is another story.'

Zenobia had already formed the impression that Madhavi's child was very fond of interrupting. Was she irritated, or captivated by the precocious questions of her husband's child? If he were her own, she might be pleased with the child's curiosity for such knowledge. But now she told him to just accept what she said. The brush-off left a peeved look on the little boy's face. Zenobia softened – 'this first creation was destroyed; it was such a very long time ago. Min's temple was there in the new age that followed. His thunderbolt shows him to be one of the sky gods, His erect phallus brings fertility.'

But not yet for me, she thought to herself. 'In these parts' she continued, 'people believe that the falcon was a gift of Min to his son Horus. Surely that is enough to satisfie even Eko's insatiable curtiosity. Eko smiled at the joke. Although Zenobia wasn't too sure if he really understood what was happening. 'Eko,' she continued, 'when you feel the sand between your toes, remember that Min lies dreaming, deep below in his splendour.'

Zenobia was anxious to get going. 'Don't worry,' she said, doing her best to keep smiling, 'there will be time to discuss all this on our journey. And oh yes' she said, 'remember, if you become separated, go to the rendezvous. You must be there before sun down or we will have to go without you.'

As the words left her mouth, Zenobia saw, with regret, the anxious look, pass over Eko's face. Had she said too much? She needed to impress the child and was in too much of a hurry for diplomacy.

Zenobia followed the sacred Temenos wall around to the northern side of the temple. A line of devotees snaked in through the smaller lintel gate that led to the Isis shrine. Avoiding this queue, Zenobia headed for the small passageway, that would let her directly to a chamber, at the back of Isis shrine. Her task was to croon softly an ancient song to the goddess, as she carefully cleaned the inner shrine of the previous evening's offerings.

Ordinary pilgrims were not allowed into the inner sanctum of the goddess. They were to stop before a latticework screen that shielded the sanctuary from the eyes of the profane. As she worked her way along, Zenobia could hear the supplications of the worshippers on the other side. Mostly in whispers, but then the voice of a Nubian, who like all of her race, seemed incapable of talking quietly even here.

'Goddess, give me back my life!'

Zenobia whispered back to her: 'why do you say you have no life?'

The Nubian lowered her voice to respond: 'Since my husband become Christian, I have no life. When we married, then we were happy. I come from Ombos…'

'The town of Seth!!' Zenobia interrupted.

'Yes Goddess, Seth's town, but do not think harshly of me for that. I threw away my necklace of carnelian beads.'

Zenobia took a sharp intake of breath in mock alarm then asked her to, 'go on.'

'The first few years of our married life was hard, but good years. We did not start a family. We were saving; using the ancient ways to stop the children coming. Then he, Ameco, my husband, he met a holy man, and we became Jacobite (she used the older term for the fashionable Christian cult). A prophet said, it was against god's will to seal the doorway to life, he said, if we do not want children, we should not lie together, but should pray and be temperate.'

'That is strange advice coming from a man!'

'Goddess, you understand how it is?'

'How many children do you have?'

'There are four in four years. Now my life is endless cooking and skivvying, while useless husband tend his flock.'

'There is more?'

'The church meets in our house. Every night people come. They, we, sing and pray late. There is food to make, more cleaning, the children.'

'What do you wish me to do?'

'My husband wants me to call the god. When people not come, he make me practice the word with him.'

'What word?'

'He say, we say, la la la, over and over and the word will come. But I try and it does not come. I hear myself only grunting like donkey in the night. What should I do?'

'Do you love your children?'

The unseen woman fell silent, 'I not say this to anyone but Goddess, I've tried ... please forgive me. What I do?'

Zenobia thought for a while. 'Leave your children with your husband, return to your home village, wait there. He will soon come to get you.'

Zenobia was already moving on, along the passageway. Snatches of conversation, barely registered in her consciousness. Then a pair of cultivated voices caught her attention, the unmistakable, effete tones, of two Roman dandies.

' . . . Who has not heard, Perseus, what monsters demented Egypt worships? One district adores the crocodile, another venerates the ibis that gorges itself with snakes. In the place where magic chords are sounded by a broken statue of Memnon, and ancient Thebes lies in ruins, men worship the glittering golden image of the long-tailed ape. In one part cats are worshipped, in another a river fish, in another whole townships venerate a dog; none adore Diana.'

'I've heard,' Perseus hissed, 'that to crunch leeks and onions is an outrage?'

'Quite, what a holy race to have such divinities springing up in their gardens!' The dandies giggled at their own joke. Then the diatribe began again.

'I also heard, my dear Juvenal, no animal that grows wool may appear upon the dinner-table; it is forbidden there to slay the young of the goat; but it is lawful to feed on the flesh of man!'

Zenobia anticipated the pause, the look of mock surprize, again the barely surpressed laughter.

'I would remind you, my dear Perseus, that when Ulysses, told a tale like this over the dinner-table, he stirred some to wrath, some perhaps to laughter, as a lying story-teller. "What?" one would say, "will no one hurl this fellow into the sea, who merits a terrible and a true Charybdis with his inventions of monstrous Laestrygones and Cyclopes? For I could sooner believe in Scylla, and the clashing Cyanean rocks and skins full of storms, or in the story how Circe, by a gentle touch, turned Elpenor and his comrades into grunting swine. Did he deem the Phaeacian people to be so devoid of brains?"'

The Greeks again cracked up with laughter. The older of

them, Juvenal, recovering, continued *soto voce*, 'By my witness – whereas the incident I shall relate, though fantastic enough, took place within recent memory, upcountry from here, an act of mob violence worse than anything in the tragedians. Search through the mythical cannons, you won't find an instance of such a collective crime. Now attend and learn what kind of novel atrocity our day and age has added to history.'

'Between the neighbouring villages of Dendara and Ombos there burns an ancient and long-cherished feud and undying hatred, whose wounds are not to be healed. Each people is filled with fury against the other because each hates its neighbours' gods, deeming that none can be held as deities save its own. So when one of these peoples held a feast, the chiefs and leaders of their enemy thought good to seize the occasion, so that their foe might not enjoy a glad and merry day.'

'I've heard,' Perseus blurted, ' that an Egyptian party can last a whole week non-stop. The Egyptians may be peasants, but for self-indulgence there's nothing – as I have observed myself, to choose between city pagiarch or barbarous peasant.'

'Indeed, Perseus, besides, victory too would be easy, it was thought, over men steeped in wine, stuttering and stumbling in their cups. On the one side were men dancing to a swarthy piper, with unguents, such as they were, and flowers and chaplets on their heads.'

'So on the other side,' Perseus, again interrupted, 'a ravenous hate?'

'Why Perseus, your eyes are sparkling, but I tell you that first comes a loud interview, a prelude to the fray: these serve as a trumpet-call to their hot passions; then shout answering shout, they charge. Bare hands do the fell work of weapons. Scarce a cheek is left without a gash; scarce one nose, if any, comes out of the battle unbroken. Through all the ranks might be seen battered faces, and features other than they were; bones gaping through torn cheeks, and fists dripping with blood from eyes!'

'As in Rome I guess they regarded the whole affair as mere horseplay, the sort of mock-battle that children engage in: what's the point of so many thousands brawling if no one gets killed?'

'Ah yes, but fiercer and fiercer grows the fight; they now search the ground for stones and hurl them against the foe. The one side, reinforced, boldly draws the sword and renews the fight with showers of arrows; the dwellers in the shady palm-groves of neighbouring Dendara turn their backs in headlong flight before the Ombite charge. Hereupon one of them, over-afraid and hurrying, tripped and was caught; the conquering host cut up his body, into a multitude of scraps and morsels and devoured it bones and all!'

'Nooo!' Perseus crooned, subconsciously looking over his shoulder, perhaps sensing that Zenobia's hidden ears were overhearing their conversation. Still Juvenal licked his lips and hissed 'There was no stewing of it in boiling pots, no roasting upon spits; they contented themselves with the corpse uncooked!'

'One should, I suppose, be grateful, Prometheus's sacred gift of fire, the spark of heaven, was spared such an outrage?'

'Yes, my dear Perseus, but I must tell you that never was flesh so relished as by those who endured to put that carcass between their teeth. For in that act of gross wickedness, do not doubt or ask whether it was only the first gullet that enjoyed its meal; for when the whole body had been consumed, those who stood furthest away actually dragged their fingers along the ground and so got a lick of the blood!'

It was the old blood libel against the followers of Seth at his ancient home at Ombos. Zenobia knew that Sethians had always eaten a small token part of their departed love ones. What these Romanised Greeks were saying, made her blood boil. She could not resist one parting shot through the grill, before she moved on:

'You Romans' she barked, 'you only ever see the faults of

others and never your own! Do you think the armed men sacrificed in your gilded arenas, are somehow nobler than rites of a simple people?'

She did not wait for a reply. A stunned silence came from the unseen deriders of their Egyptian hosts.

Zenobia was moving on, down the hidden corridor, heading for the chamber behind the shrine of Min.

A great throng of pilgrims filled the courtyard beyond the grill. It was difficult to see, but Zenobia thought she could make out the heads of Jeuy the Diviner, his large arms curved out like a bull's horns, to make a space in front of his body, for Madhavi's child.

Suddenly a strange feeling came over her - an spontaenous feeling of irritation as if something had latched onto her uninvited. With a sharp out breath, almost a sneeze, Zenobia hissed 'get from me!'

The curse sent Jay's spirit careering through the lattice work. Now suddenly she could view everything from Eko's diminutive vantage point. Jeuy's voice was bellowing in his ear:

'Hold it up, the offering, hold it up, good lad.'

Eko was struggling. Jeuy mumbling his prayers, most of which were meant for the god but landed in Eko's ear.

Min stood there in his splendour, seven foot tall. Eko's eye was immediately drawn to the erect phallus. It rose straight out from the centre of his belly. He knew a man's prick was different to a boy's, but really Min's, it was so much bigger than his own. Waking in the night to pass water, his little todger hardly matched up. Would his one day be like that?

A shudder ran through him. It wasn't even wrought from the same cool limestone, as the rest of Min's body. It was the wrong colour. Why did it look like that? He saw how it came away. Was it true that Isis borrowed it, when she made love to the corpse of Osiris, emasculated by Seth? Did she have need of such a stout peg? Eko's arms ached from holding forth the little ceremonial loaves, the greenery of the lettuce, and the tiny grail of beer that in the melee had mostly slopped away.

A vast sigh went through the crowd. Min rocked visibly forward on his marble plinth. Affirmation. Silence followed by a crump, as Min settled back on his feet. The repeated movement. Min nodding to the crowd, a second time, then a third.

'Count them!' Jeuy bellowed in his ear. Eko was looking for his aunt. He'd decided she was a nice person, if a little whimsical. Whimsical was one of his father Philo's words - Eko wasn't too sure what it meant, he just liked the sound of it. Where was she, Zenobia? She said she'd be somewhere nearby in the temple. Zenobia had instructed them if the god rocked to count the times . Three times this happened. Three days and they would be leaving. That's what it meant. The priests were moving though the temple, driving them out to make way for another batch of supplicants. Shaking their rattles to hurry the crowds out, grabbing any offerings not deposited at the feet of the god.

The priest grabbed Eko's offerings, spilling the beer. Jeuy ignored them. He lifted the boy up like a sack, and shouldered his way from the temple.

6   Lost

Outside again. 'Jeuy,' Eko asked bashfully, 'do all men have such magnificent private parts?'

'Well my son,' he smiled, 'not all are so blessed, he is a god!'

'Even the evil one, Seth?' Jeuy's smile turned to a frown. 'What you know of Seth?'

But before Eko could answer, the vision faded. Jay was herself, lying on her hospital bed. A nurse was holding a cup of tea to her lips, asking if she felt better. 'You delirious for days, the medicine does this.'

Jay was drifting. She thought she should try to focus on something else – resist the temptation to dissociate again back to Zenobia's adventure in Koptos. She needed her own memories running through her head. Something to think about, in her world. A job interview – would that be banal enough?

Jay recalled an interview for a small scholarship from the Wellcome Trust. She never got the job, her face didn't fit, wrong accent, wrong school. She'd taken the bus from Oxford to London. Her proposed project was on ancient Egyptian medicine. Now she remembered that lovely summer day. She'd arrived in London with hours to spare before the interview. The City Link set everyone down at Marble Arch. There was time for a walk across the park.

Hyde park was crowded with early picnickers, joggers, dog-walkers, skaters, pram-pushers and riders. She meandered for half an hour until she stood beneath the vast Victorian space-rocket that is the Albert Memorial. From here Exhibition Road led down to the Victoria and Albert museum. The V&A was the quintessential museum of the British Empire. It did, so she remembered, have just one unusual Egyptian artefact. A wand of Seth, donated by Flinders Petrie. There was plenty of time for Jay to go take a look.

It was just ten o'clock. The doors of the museum were opening to the handful of early visitors. She could smell the floor polish, as she swept through the quiet galleries, heading for the restaurant. She picked up a map from reception and looked at it over her coffee. None of the entries mentioned anything Egyptian. She'd have to ask.

Confusion at the information desk. They had never heard of such a thing. Was it sculpture or metalwork? How large was it?

Jay wasn't sure. Maybe she'd just explore and see if she could find it. Maybe she'd got it all wrong. Parting shot from receptionist: 'Try Islamic ceramics, room 182, sixth floor.'

'Yeah, I'll do that'.

The lift doors opened onto a deserted ceramics gallery. The words from Omar Khyam flashed into her mind, provoking a wry smile: 'many a beauty destined to bloom unseen in the desert air.'

Jay scanned the floorplan then wheeled right into a long, narrow gallery. The golden sunlight streamed beneficently from the skylights. The pots aged visibly as she walked - modern, then British, European, Renaissance, now Islamic. She paused, running her fingers over a rough terracotta olive jar, Greek or Cretan? She walked on, her eyes falling on greens and yellows.

Now the pots from every case were blue, everything was blue. The fragments, must be old, special in some way. Arabic writing – the name of god, blue-green patterns, maybe from the wall of an old mosque. Jay reached the last of hundreds of teak and glass cabinets.

'Seth' she thought to herself, 'I know you're here somewhere, I can feel you.' She paused 'but where are you?'

Looking back, her breath caught in her lungs. There he was. Her body tingled. Seth did not share his case with another – centred and solitary he stood, out of sight until one looked backwards, was this god, concealed in more ways that one, truly the Hidden God - was, is, always shall be.

Seth's all seeing, inscrutable gaze fell on her. Taller than her by more than a foot, his downward curving snout, massively thick like a hippopotamus. Tiny arms, square cut ears hidden beneath his massive, domed, fez-like head. His body, a stout column, adorned with hieroglyphs, the triple name of a king. The curve of the hips, the stubby legs. Lines of black raindrops flowing over Seth's body. Under the lines of paint, the lustrous faience blue, still stunning after the six thousand years since the sceptre was buried in Ombos, Seth's town.

Desert sand and natron. Jay stared up at a mouth, which stretched and crinkled into a sardonic smile. Her eyes met the hooded gaze of the god, and the words 'Be not unaware of me O Nephthys, if you know me then I shall know you,' echoed through the gallery.

Instinctively the traditional response formed in Jay's mind. It burst forth in Zenobia's fine voice:

'Be not unaware of me O Seth,

if you know me then I shall know you'

'Where are we?'

'At the faience kilns, waiting for uncle Jeuy.'

'I'm bored.'

'Rest a little longer, till it is the time to move.'

'I miss my mother, where is she?'

Zenobia, her mind preoccupied with other things, nevertheless did her best to sound optimistic. 'Try not to think about it. Madhavi and your father, will meet us in Berenice!'

But Eko though he detected a tension in Zenobia's voice. Eko thought to himself how confusing were the relationships between his mother, his father and this woman, aunt Zenobia. He did not understand it completely, but already knew enough, that it was best to change the subject, or the blood was likely to drain from Zenobia's face, and she would become distant and sarcastic about his father.

'How far is Berenice?' He already knew the answer. He also knew how asking the same question over and over was likely to be irritating. But Eko wanted to change the subject.

'Eko darling, I've told you that a hundred times already. Berenice is two weeks camel ride from here,' her voice softening, taking on a resigned tone as she spoke. 'We will be moving soon. Riding all night. The vanguard of the caravan is already working its way up the cliff pass. We must wait our turn to be loaded.'

They were to travel in one of the night caravans. This was a relatively comfortable option considering the time of year – the Messore, when the sun god Ra is at his very strongest. The nights would be cool, perhaps even chilly. The days would be spent huddled with their goods in the almost unbearable, stifling heat, looking for shade, not moving, trying to sleep.

'I know,' Eko dissembled, 'But what then, at the end of the road, Berenice, what's there, are we to set up house?'

'The first ship of the season is awaiting us.' Zenobia stopped short, not meaning to say so much.

'Ship! What ship?'

'Nothing, just a figure of speech.' Now Zenobia was dissembling, 'no one travels this road unless bound outward, through the Red Sea to the ports beyond.'

The lines of the contract ran through Zenobia's mind: 'I will give to your camel driver 170 Talents, 50 drachmas, for the use of the road to Berenice.' Zenobia's signature was here. 'I, the illegible agent's name, will convey your goods inland through the desert under guard and under security to the public warehouses for receiving revenues at Berenice'. This much, Zenobia had told to Eko. But the contract went further: 'and I will place them under your ownership and seal until loading aboard at the Gulf, and I will load them aboard, at the required time, on a seaworthy boat, on the Gulf, and I will convey them across the Maes Erythraim stream to the warehouse that receives them at Musiris, and I will similarly place them under the ownership of you or your representative etcetera, etcetera, etcetera.'

Zenobia had made this contract with one of those western merchants, who in the words of some local poet, 'go out with gold and return with pepper.' The trade did not make sense but who was arguing. It is not as if a perfectly fine pepper does not grow here. But there is a taste amongst the Romans for the foreign stuff.

The company's ship is already bobbing at its mooring. She'll be a real monster, that a few weeks earlier decanted 400 tons of cargo from her lead lined holds. Some to be stored in the company's warehouse, but most caravanned across the desert to Koptos, to be loaded aboard new ships. In the old days, two such shipments would have yielded almost 20,000 talents - 30 million denarii. It is said that Augustus once used this money, to give every one of Rome's half a million citizens, a cash dole, worth a month's salary for the average man in the street. In those days, 120 such ships made the journey each season. That was a lot of cargo on the move.

'Foul Bay', or Berenice, so they say, is named after Ptolemy Philadelpus's mum. To journey across the desert is long and perilous. But Berenice is 240 miles closer to the mouth of the Erythraen, the 'red' seas. Foul winds blow relentlessly down the Gulf from the North. These winds blow continuously for ten months of the year. They are the fiercest in the known world, as every resident of Berenice can testify. Even seasoned navigators fear this passage. Ships that push on the 240 miles to the 'mussel harbour', Myos Hormos, face a tough end to their journey.

Most of those luxury goods that pass down Pan's Road, are from India, some by the direct route, others in the holds of smaller ships, that sail out to meet Indian vessels at some entrepot midway. At the beginning of the season, a score or more local Beja headsmen, subcontract their camels and herdsmen. Each chiefdon sends a minimum of twenty 'Delta' camels, to work Pan's Road for several months. It's a golden triangle, Berenice to Koptos, Koptos to Myos Hormos, then along the coast to Berenice. Only now the traffic is all one way, away from Koptos.

The strange beasts are the most efficient way to haul cargo across the desert. At a push they can go days without water, for they are habituated to very harsh conditions, that would kill almost any other beast. Their herders are young and tough. They will make a good account of themselves if there is trouble. The Beja say the beasts are beautiful. Their prehensile lips are a parody of some gap toothed whore, her dark lascivious eyes dripping with kohl.

7 Camels

All around is the clamorous moaning of the camels as sack after backbreaking sack is hoisted up on their packsaddles. Such overloading means they will walk slowly, need extra food and watering.

For now the Camels are frisky in the cool night air. By daytime they will conserve their energy, desperately trying to avoid dehydration. As night falls they long for nothing more than endless hours foraging on low-grade scrub. A camel dreams of his favourite forage - wild peas, or the distinctive spreading crown of the all giving acacia. The resinous Egyptian thorn, sweet smelling indigo, frankincense, myrrh, or capper plants. In between the bigger trees, the camels instinctively hunts down veiny, shrublets of spiny *Ziziphus*. In season the plant holds a tiny edible secret in its five petaled, bisexual flowers. Men watch them, shouting 'ghot', 'gut' and 'quud', driving the camels way from the multi-branched, evergreen spiny shrub. Man and camel want those fruits that look like sweet dates, their brittle coats enclosing a brown-gray sticky pulp. Or the Persica, the sacred tree of Osiris. The pubescent evergreen tree whose fibrous twigs leave the camel's mouth feeling fresh and salty.

On the march the camels must content themselves with a snatched mouthful of bitter drupe or of purple bunch grass, stipa or dry tussocks of panicum, inedible by any other beast but a camel.

Caravans travel at night making camp well before the first hints of green dawn breaks over the bleak, jagged masses of rock that flank the Nile valley. Night hunting birds return to their roosts. Rudely awakened gulls shriek, turning a beady eye on the company. Beyond is nothing but a boundless expanse of gravel. Out of the frying pan of Koptos and into the fire of the desert they go.

Already Zenobia is longing for her home, to wash the fine dust from her skin with the rich opaque water of the Nile.

Pan's Road – as the Greeks call ancient Min, the god of male procreative power. From a desert hideout he is watching them. His phallus is erect. He is in front of his hut, close to his kitchen garden of succulent lettuce plants. Nearby is Isis, the wife of Min.

Min's lordship over the desert compels all travellers to

break their journey at his shrine just outside of the cultivated area. Here, all must pray to the god, for a safe passage through his realm; for protection from the harsh desert conditions; for sanctuary from the roving brigands, that are a permanent hazard on the journey.

Before the god, Jay closes her eyes for a moment of silent prayer. She opens them to stare at the ceiling of the hospital ward. A nurse is asking her if she wants something.

'No' she croaks.

'But you spoke in your sleep of Zenobia.'

'I did?'

'Yes, Zenobia, it's the name of a shop.'

Ignoring her, Jay fell into an incoherent ramble of how after the Palmyrene rebellion, Koptos fell to the Blemmyes. 'The Romans fear them', she said, 'they say these ancient Nubian tribesmen are headless; their eyes and mouth are placed in the breast!'

'Are you feeling better?' the nurse croons. The nurse, knowing that Jay will soon come to her senses, ignore's what her patient has just said. The nurse repeats her question: 'Did she want anything, from the shop?'

'No thank you. Are there any messages for me?'

The nurse went away to find out. Leaving Jay to recall how the Zenobia food chain took its name from the famous warrior queen, whose family were traders from Palmyra. The nurse returned with an aerogramme that bore an Indian postmark.

A friendly letter from her friend Murugan in India. But Jay's eyes would not focus for more than a few moments.

'Would you like me to read it?' the kindly nurse asked inquisitively.

'No, it's alright. I'll finish it later. Her eyes fell on 'As I understand it the 'Pattini scroll' once in my possession, was a collection of five distinct ancient manuscripts. One of these is a personal account of the migration of various members of a family of traders, from their ancestral home on the banks of the Nile. Well let us assume that their home was in Koptos. Was it not from this place that trading expeditions were organised across the desert to the Red Sea coast? From the Red Sea ports of Myos Hormos and Berenice, goods and people took sail, on the favourable Hippalos wind, that took them, by forty days and nights, to landfall on the extreme south of India, in ancient Musiris, near to modern day port of Colchin. Not so far from where I now live!'

8   On Pan's Road

Eko's body ached from the first night of bouncing on the back of a donkey, as it made its way across the cultivated area, up the steep mountain pass to the high desert proper. Bleak, jagged masses of rock, flanked the fertile valley of the Nile. Beyond was nothing but a boundless expanse of red gravel. Vultures circles overhead. Out of the frying pan of Koptos into the fire of the desert.

The wise donkey keeps a judicious gap between itself and the large shuffling feet of the trudging camels, who were more than capable of biting a spiteful lump from its neck.

They set the pace, half a watch at a steady if complaining trudge of four miles per hour. On a good run they would cover sixteen miles. The night after tomorrow they would arrive at Phenicon, at the intersection between the two great desert roads – the Myos Hormos Road, the route of legendary Queen Hatshepsut's to the treasure-lands of exotic Punt.

Pan's Road is the long way across the desert to the very mouth of the Red Sea at Berenice. Between them and Phenicon lay a day's stop over at a walled hydreumata, built by the Romans. It, like many of the smaller stone watchtowers they had passed in the darkness, were now under the control of the Beja.

Just before dawn Eko is roused from his stupor by Zenobia's shaking. They were within sight of Matula hydreumata, but the caravan had stopped at a remote Paneion. The camels were anxious to be off-loaded and forage for food. It was a good sign. No one wanted to see overworked animals, hot, tired, disgruntled, making for the nearest shade, too listless to forage for food. If the camels lost condition they could easily become a liability on the journey ahead. Without them their prospects were bleak. Almost as quickly as Eko's beast was hobbled, it extended its neck and hared off to investigate a nearby acacia.

Custom dictated that during their stop all travellers must supplicate the desert god, making offerings for safe passage in the days to come. The Paneion was little more than a great pile of smooth granite boulders. A cave, hidden below ground level, is a small spring that never ran dry. Above them, a giant stone perched like loose tooth in its socket, able to rock back and forth. No one knew or cared, whether this prodigy, was the reason all here must now pray to the great god Pan. They just had to do it.

There were many such rocky outcrops in a desert honeycombed with caves and passages. The desert dwellers know every one. Too small to be an oasis, they could support a small band of men, hiding in the deep desert awaiting the opportunity to steal a sheep, a female camel or maybe even an unattended child. Unfortunates then to be taken southwards and sold into slavery.

The logan stone showed no sign of movement to Eko's touch. Like the statues in the temple, such a rock will often nod its answer to a question. This one needed a stronger impetuous. Something pricked a cell of memory in Eko's brain. An image of himself as a small child, slipping unnoticed and ignored into the temple, there to observe the wag priests in the house of Min.

He knew the secret of their signs. Every year on the god's birthday, his splendour was taken out of the temple into the swirling crowds of pilgrims. It was a great game during which one party yelled insults at another, as they elbowed their way to the best position before the god.

The space immediately in front of the palanquin is empty but for several petitioners waiting for a pause, the opportunity to ask a question of the god. Limpet like, Eko clung close to one of eight image bearers of the god. When one of them dipped ever so slightly, the god slipped forward, nodded his answer. An accidental stumble, made the god's head fall backwards, meaning no.

The stone and rocks of nearby desert are decorated with wonderful stele. Eko hears a dissembodied voice describe them as crude. Eko does not understand how they can be crude. They all show the image of Min. His thing protrudes. The god stands canopied under the outstretched wings of the sun. On his head, a plummed headdress with nestling solar disk. The god's right arm is flung backwards as if about to strike with his flail. His left arm disappears behind the inscription. The gesture is strange. Eko wants to ask Zenobia what it means; she is sure to know.

Indeed Zenobia's follows the familiar lineaments of the god Min, as he makes the gesture, so familiar to her, from sight of it several times each day in the House of Life. The House of Life, place of priestly instruction, the locus of the mysteries of Hekau, the oldest of all the magicians.

Eko mimicks the gesture, his hands flying to the right, then the left outwards. He bows, then straightens, reaching upwards into what becomes a wide yawn.

Aromatic incense burns on a waist high thurible. Everyone can smell it. Jeuy, trying hard to be helpful, to teach his new protégé something, mumbles how all temples have an insatiable appetite for incense. How it is dragged down Pan's Road by the ton. He reaches into his robe for a small bag of the stuff; replenishing the smoking coals with the fresh frankincense the God loves so much.

Eko's nostrils fill with the smell of old stones from the portals of time. The melancholic Greek inscription fills him with sadness. It is not the tongue of his mother. Tears spring to his eyes as he thinks of Madhavi, wondering where she might be; when she will come to reclaim him? These people are kind, his aunt Zenobia doing her best to hide her true feelings. Does she really like him? Does she really want him here? He just can't tell. He misses home. The likeness of his mother's beautiful face dances before him, mouthing words in a strange language, willing him to understand. But he cannot.

He reads the inscription, much worn by desert sandstorms, but still legible. 'Paid for by Gaius Cominus Leugas, set there many years ago in the 23rd of Thoth in the eighteenth year of the reign of Claudius.' Gaius, the imperial geographer, thanks Pan, guardian of the eastern desert, for a particularly valuable outcrop of porphyrites. So this is where is comes from, that purple stone horded and monopolized by the Romans. 'Be good' or the Romans will come; force you to drag it from the quarries to the river. You good for nothing but a galley slave, rowing across the sea to Rome.

In the melée a man stands aside, watching but not making any obvious sign of devotion to the desert protector. He is Hephaestus, a name imprinted in everyone's ears from the moment the caravan overseer bellowed it out. A beardless eunuch, which is *how I would be*, thinks Eko, were I ever cut for the southern slave markets. Although he is not too sure what it all means.

But something about Hephaestus disturbs him; he seems neither one thing nor another. Though still handsome, he is no longer a boy. Perhaps he is a songster. Is he destined to sing in the evening entertainments of some Indian king? If so, one day he must return, when his voice fails, or his master grows tired of his blandishments.

Eko is intrigued at his obvious irreligion, the stranger's open contempt for the shrine. Perhaps he is a Christian – if so then he needs no warning of the dangerous times to come. The Romans will have none of the Palestinian troublemakers anywhere near their quarries. Many a sad cargo walked these roads before the Beja drove the Romans out. Schoolboy stories of prisoners with eyes gouged, hamstrings cut, transported to the banks of the Red Sea. Then back to the land from whence they came, to some grim but short future existence.

Madhavi, Eko's natural mother, encouraged him to study in his schoolbooks, the works of the Greek navigator Hippalos. Perhaps she knew something of their final destination. Eko loved the stories, descriptions that floated like bubbles into his memory. Would he ever see the 'coast marked by clusters of mean huts of the Ichthypagoi, the eaters of fish, and inland from these where villages and pastures of folk who speak two languages but who are vicious and cruel. They who plunder any who stray from a course down the middle and enslave any they rescue from shipwreck. Any course down this Arabia coast is full of risk, if only for its lack of harbours, poor anchorages or foul rocky stretches with no approach because of cliffs. They are fearsome in every respect.'

Eko leaves the shrine in time to see Hephaestus questioned by some official. He reaches into his robe for a fragment of pottery ostraker, on which is his written authorisation for the journey. He drops his pack and sits. The fine desert dust has found the creases of his ragged clothes. But rags do not always signify poverty. Zenobia has made them all wear worn but comfortable clothes. Modest clothing so as not to draw the attention of thieves or pickpockets. With home in sight, they each had something smart in their packs. It was the seasoned traveller's way.

Hephaestus' neck was muddied with his own perspiration,

but bore the unmistakable whiteness of a eunuch, that no amount of sun could darken.

He looked up and fixed Eko with smiling eyes.

Eko returned the welcoming look, taking it as a sign to move closer. 'Where are you heading' he asks? Eko lies, deflecting a question, whose answer must already be obvious, saying that he didn't really know.

Smiling knowingly, Hephaestus turns the question upon himself, 'I am returning to Balgazza' he says naming a mysterious savage sounding place. Eko thinks he may have heard of it. Something in his manner says it will be a long time, perhaps days, before he reaches the place.

'Why are you going there?'

Hephaestus hesitates.

On impulse, Eko pumps him for more information: 'I won't tell anyone. . . but are you a Christian?'

It was an impertinent question even for a child – if true, the subject would find it difficult to deny in good conscious, but such an admission could be dangerous, especially if the Romans were returning.

Eko slides even closer, positioning himself beside his new friend, hoping for more gossip.

With a sign of resignation Hephaestus admits 'Yes I am.'

Eko recalls that Christians feel a compulsion to testify. Always curious, Eko contemplates how he should tempt

Hephaestus to spill the beans. It will be child's play to have him sing like a canary. Adopting his most winsome manner, Eko asks 'Will you tell me your story?'

The defeated Christian sighs and with hardly any hesitation, gives a rapid résumé of his life thus far.

9   Hephaestus' tale

Hephaestus had travelled throughout the empire for many years. His goal now was to get as far away from Rome as possible. Journey's end was to be Musiris in the south of India. At Musiris he knew there to be a small Christian community founded by the apostle Tomas the 'doubter'.

Eko's expression changed from wide eyed encouragement to blank incomprehension. Hephaestus needed to explain more of this Tomas, a name, of which, he had to admit, the world was ignorant. 'Here' he said, holding up a small scroll, 'this is his book' he paused, 'imperfect and full of exaggerated embellishments it undoubtedly is. But it is his book nonetheless.' Hephaestus looked pleased with himself. Eko, still somewhat blank, asked what was it about, 'is it a good story?'

Hephaestus cleared his throat as if about to say something very important. 'Well yes', he said, 'it is a good story, although that hardly seems to say it all.' He smiled, subverting his own portentous tone. 'It tells,' he continued, 'of how a merchant called Habbanes bought him, Tomas that is, from Jesus the carpenter.'

'Tomas was a slave?' Eko interjected, trying to be helpful.

'Yes indeed,' Hephaestus agreed, 'Tomas was a slave. And he was taken, no doubt down this very road, to India, where he came across a Jewish girl in the King's court. And,' He said, pausing for effect, 'during the period of his stay there, several Jewish people were converted to Christianity.'

Eko seemed unimpressed, barely able to hide a yawn. Ignoring this Hephaestus ploughed on, determined to finish his story.

'He established seven and a half churches with 75 Brahmin families as teachers and over 3000 converts!'

'What,' Eko snorted, 'what does it mean, seven and a half churches?'

Hephaestus is stung. His tone now uncertain: 'The seven churches are theirs in entirety, the half church, at Musiris, is shared with others.'

'You're making this up!' Eko quipped, using a favourite expression of his father's. A moment later the reminder caused a shadow to pass over his heart. He felt guilty that he had not thought of his real family for several hours. Forgetting them might put them in peril. Hephaestus, knowing none of this, continued:

'These new converts were called Tomas Christians. And before you ask, Tomas was martyred, just four years after Peter, by a fanatic at the place of rock. His followers took his body, burying him in the tombs of the Chiefs. Until one day, a Syrian merchant exhumed his body, and took it to Edessa where it is still entombed and venerated.'

Sensing the change in Eko's mood, Hephaestus put his scroll away. 'that's a big bite to be going on with – why don't you tell me something about Eko?'

'Oh I dunno?' Eko felt awkward, as if confiding in this stranger was somehow to be disloyal to his parents, whose whereabouts were a mystery. 'Come on,' Hephaestus persists, 'fair is fair. Tell me about yourself, who you are?'

'Who I am?' Eko repeats the question, 'that's a funny question, what does it mean *who you are*? It's obvious, I'm Eko, son of,' he pauses, 'Philo by his' again he pauses, then the difficult word, 'concubine, my mother Madhavi.'

'Ah,' Hephaestus takes up the thread, 'so the people I've seen you with, are they your mother and father?'

'That's Zenobia, she is not my mother, although she is, was married to Philo, my father. My true father and my mother are in Alexandria.'

Hephaestus kept his face turned towards the earth, saying nothing, just listening. 'But', Eko continued, 'Madhavi will meet me at Berenice, and everything will be good. She will take a different route across this desert. We shall all be together there.'

'So you have two mothers? Many would envy you for that.'

'Yes maybe, but... but it makes me confused sometimes.' After a pause he added 'Zenobia, my aunt, I'm not sure that she likes me, likes me being here that is.'

Hephaestus turned his kind eyes upwards, 'Eko, I should think so. Looks to me like she is a happy enough person, all things considering. She seems to like you well enough. Even I, a complete stranger, can see it.'

Eko blushed but did not reply. Hephaestus repeated himself, this time as a question, 'I think she likes you very much?'

Eko had to reply 'yes, part of me thinks that too.'

'*Part of you*, are you accustomed to think of yourself as all broken up into parts inside?'

It was an odd question. Eko didn't quite know how to answer. 'Well yes, is that not how you feel? It's like there are two different people inside me – one the boy Eko and the other...' he paused.

'Yes,' Hephaestus said, 'go on, you can trust me.'

'I've never told anyone this, but since starting this journey, I've felt something else, like there *is* someone else inside. And this person, I don't know their name … ' Eko was too embarrassed to go on.

'Don't worry Eko, I won't tell anyone your secret. I can help you, if I tell you that others have experienced this.'

Eko wasn't at all sure he wanted help, but replied: 'Do you feel this way?'

'Not quite as you, but yes I understand.'

'Thank you. But can we stop talking about it now, finish *your* story . . please.'

'OK, where were we? I was telling you of our holy man Tomas. Well Tomas wondered through many lands, until he found a people among whom philosophical doubt was second nature.'

'But' Eko interjected, 'I hear the Indians are very religious people . . . after the fashion of barbarians.'

'Indeed' Hephaestus replied, 'but am I right in supposing you are from Alexandria?'

Eko nodded.

'Then you will have seen the Indian gymnosophists, the selfsame who stood naked before Alexander, making such monkeys of their Greek brethren?'

Eko laughed.

'Well.' Hephaestus smiled, 'take it from me; there are

many kinds of naked philosophers in India. It is truly a country addicted to philosophical disputation, to rational doubt. I shall be very happy there.'

Hephaestus was still smiling, but the anxious look on Eko's face, spoke of doubt, of a future in such far off strange lands.

'Travelling is expensive' Hephaestus said 'and I do not have much money. If I ever return I shall have to work my way back via the coastal route, no doubt the guest of some barbarous town, where work can be had by one such as I.'

'What do you do?' Eko asked, wondering whether his religion might be a ready source of cash.

'I have always been able to sing. I shall earn my keep providing simple evening entertainments, perhaps translating or teaching the Greek and Latin tongues to the barbarians.'

Then he too looked sad, his eyes over moist, like many; he was nostalgic for his former life in the wonderful city. 'I don't expect I shall return or see my beloved Alexandria. I have liquidated all my assets. I just hope for news of my old friend and companion Pelagius.

'From Alexandria?' Eko asked.

'No, not he – he came from the edge of the known world - but he was a great sophist nonethless – he came from the most provincial of places, a mean, backward, tiny little island called Britannia.'

Eko had not heard of such a place. Inwardly he searched his list of most mysterious of places. 'Was it' he said finally, 'like Thule.' But Hephaestus was sunk in thought. Just when Eko was beginning to feel ignored he continued saying what to Eko was a very odd thing:

'Eko, you are just beginning your life, mine is more than half over. Should you ever meet one such as I again, I hope the experience will be good.'

Eko was puzzled as to why it should not be. Everything so far showed his new Christian friend to be a good fellow, a bit serious maybe, but such was often the way with adults.

'Sometimes,' Hephaestus explained, 'My fellow believers fill me with shame. The new age prophised by so many holy men and women never did come, so now they turn on everyone. When it suits them they back the Romans. They have even looted temples, burned many books. It was not meant to be this way. If you should ever suffer at the hands of them, it may be some compensation to know, that I know what it's like. The church reserve their worst for those who they feel have erred within their own ranks. They prefer heathens to their own rebels. I too have been on the receiving end. It was not meant to be so, no it was not meant to be so.'

He stopped talking.

'Cheer up,' Eko said, sensing it was his turn to be positive, 'things will get better. That's what my father always says.'

'Yes,' Hephaestus agreed. But they both knew more than they cared to say. Knew well enough that they were all little more than refugees.

It was Eko who broke the spell, 'Tell me more about your friend Pelagius. Was he a fisherman?'

'Ah Pelagius!' just saying the name made Hephaestus eyes light up. 'No, he was never a fisherman. No, he was one of the Celtoi, converted to the faith by Aaron the prophet. He was a handsome man, fairer and taller than most Romans. His Celtish name meant 'from the sea' He once told me a legend, that all the folk of his tribe actually *lived* in the sea. They mated with humankind in some distant time. Let me tell you that he was said to be one of the greatest living thinkers.'

Eko snorted but bit his tongue, asking instead who were the others?

'One,' continued Hephaestus, hardly noticing Eko's scepticism, 'the other is Jerome, who lives not too far from here, in a hermitage in the desert near Elephantine. Another is Augustine, who also hails from *Africa*. But,' he paused, 'I do not like either of them much.'

Eko looked relieved.

'Pelagius was always clearer to me.'

The sun by this time was already high in the sky. Eko remembered he should be back. He might have spent too much time away from Zenobia and Jeuy. They could be looking, urging him to eat, then rest, before the evening march. Sensing Hephaestus was perhaps warming too much to his topic, he willed him to be quick. 'I oughta go.' he said lamely.

'OK, my little friend, perhaps we shall talk again later?'

'Yes' he said, 'I'd like that.'

'Remember one thing,'

'Yes what?'

'Ama et quod fac vis"

'Yes' he said, 'I will remember, are those the words of your friend?'

Hephaestus nodded.

'I shall remember, *ama et quod fac vis*.

'Do you know what it means?'

'Yes, of course, love and do what you will!'

Eko glanced back as he walked away. Hephaestus was already lying facedown, desert fashion on a mat, he would soon be asleep.

So too would Eko.

10   Caesura

Mid afternoon. Smoke rising from the company's cooking fires, drifted across the encampment, into Eko's nostrils. Great cauldrons of the traveller's staple diet were on the boil. Zenobia had already collected their ration of the ubiquitous millet porridge. It was the basis of the evening meal, supplemented, if you were wise, by whatever extras shared the precious space in one's pack. The navvies were already reloading the camels in readiness for the night march across the desert to the next hydreumata. The caravan would not arrive until the rising sun was in their face, and the heat, thereafter to be unbearable, was mild and welcoming. Soon they would all be walking out of the dusk into the coolness of the night. The end of the night's labour, the promise of a fresh drink at Phoenicon. As the hours pass, all would look anxiously ahead for signs of the fort, with its precious watering place.

Zenobia was gossiping with a Roman woman, whose superfluous cooking fire, shared the same rocky shelter. 'Famine food', she hissed, indicating the mess of porridge, dished out by the workers of the caravanserai.

'It be boiled four times in new water. Dried in the sun, ground to flour and reduced to porridge. Kisra would have been better,' she said, using the word for flat bread or cake. 'Not enough millet', she complained, pulling a face and throwing down her bowl.

Eko was hungry. Bitter or not, he finished his ration.

Eko lay listening, quietly, his mind hardly focussing on their words. The widow had spent most of her life in one or other of the stations along the road. Before the Beja drove away the Roman garrisons, she had accompanied her husband, a retired legionnaire, to the little desert fort, hardly more than a fortified villa. The Beja had let them both stay unmolested. Her husband died there of natural causes. So she was a widow longing now to return to her family, in a small village outside Rome. If she could just get to them, through all this chaos, all would be well.

The widow told Zenobia that the road ahead was called Camel Pass. Nearby was the entrance to another wadi, that led further into the desert towards the east. Above them, in the south, rose the high peaks of Mount Hamad.

The ochre tops of the mountain were still bathed in the final rays of daylight. Her rugged slopes were already in evening shade. The widow talked of how, even when the first stars appeared in the sky, her husband's work was not at an end. There was always some cargo to discharge into the magazines of the bleak Roman fort. New cargoes to supervise. Always shouting, as the camels waiting impatiently for their turn at the water troughs, that had to be filled with water from the deep bore-well.

Apart from her husband, they employed several people, often local prisoners, who had received a sentence for some misdemeanour or other. They became part of the work levy for the watering station. After years of work they would be allowed to return across the desert to their herds and family.

The widow's old hydreumata was further ahead in the desert at Porsou. Now it was a ruin. Not because of the Beja, just the collapse of the walls of the well. When all this is over, the Romans will send a new man, a Markus or a Gaius, to their old house. The Markus will arrive with his family, to take over at the end of the season. He will be inexperienced and untried. He will be like my husband was when young. Slightly anxious, trying his damnest to conceal the fact.

As she spoke, Eko raised himself on one elbow. She was

stuck in the past, he thought. But she, seeing him thus, pushed into his hand a little dried meat and bread.

'My husband' she continued, 'was planning to send a work detail to repair that well. We had to wait on the arrival of an experienced engineer via Berenice to supervise. His job was to run an efficient station. Everything, locking down at night, so that any marauders would not have access to the water. When there was real trouble, we had to hold out until daylight. Help would come. When Rome was here,' she said lowering her voice; 'no bandit ever attacked the forts. They were like pearls strung along Pan's Road. A little thieving, that was the worst of it. The real danger's out there,' she said, pointing out to the open desert. 'Out there,' she said, 'there are bandit villages hidden up in mountain strongholds. The Barbaroi or Troglodytes. They would not dare attack us directly. They just bide their time, watching through the night. Sometimes a young man rustles one of the camels, proving himself. Or,' she said, letting her beady eye fall on Eko, 'they look for young boys, to sell in the slave markets down south.' She was looking directly at him, smacking her lips, her face cracked by a wicked smile.

Zenobia snapped out of the mood first. 'Come on' she said, 'we must get packed up and ready to go. It cannot be more than half of the hour before the foreman will be signalling the start.' She scanned the camp for Jeuy. Then under her breath, she told herself he must have gone off into the gloom, to find a private place for his ablutions? Surely he was ready by now? With instructions for Eko to pack but stay near the bags, she would go across into a nearby wadi, answer the call of nature herself, find Jeuy.

Zenobia couldn't find him amongst the thicket. The place was deserted. She quickly drew up her dress and squatted to let loose a great gush of urine.

She found herself peering though the acacia scrub. There *was* someone there. He hadn't seen her but there, just yards away in the gloom, Jeuy was busily cleaning his skin. Water was too precious for washing, instead he was rubbing his skin with vigorous handfuls of absorbent *fuller's* clay. Zenobia could only admire the results, as Jeuy worked his way across his entire body, turning first one way, then another. Jeuy's skin was perfect, a tribute to his devotions at the shrine of Narcissus, afterall, priests were the *Hem Neteru*, literally those that cleansed the divine clothes and body of the gods, with the same fuller's clay?

Jeuy finished his ablutions, rinsing his mouth with a tiny sip of water, cleaning his teeth with a fresh stick of kat and then running an ivory comb through his thick hair before, still half naked, deftly rebraiding it.

This done he rose quickly, adjusted his clothes, looked

around and moved off into the night. Zenobia waited another moment, then stood shakily to her feet, smoothing the fabric of her garment into place. She walked back to their luggage; drawing up her veil to hide any knowing that might be in her eyes.

In the time between Zenobia and Jeuy's return, Eko had fallen into an rapid fire argument with the widow – asking her to explain why the god's allow bad things to happen. She was not quite up to the challenge. Zenobia interrupted with her own nostrum: 'The gods are not so powerful'.

11 Kamsin

Ahead of them stretched the body of Geb. Above was the glowing skin of his amorous sister Nuit. No moon but the stars so close. The initial excitement of the journey forgotten, replaced by apprehension and the toil over a dark desert road. The camels growled, slapping their big feet on the gravel. Underneath the nervous anxiety of the travellers, lay a genetic fear of the desert. Out in the darkness, nameless demons were waited patiently for their moment.

Despite a day's fitful sleep under the sun, the body's natural rhythm always asserted itself. It was so difficult to keep awake. Jeuy, walking beside Eko's donkey, for the umpteenth time pointing out interesting features in the sky, testing him.

'There' he said. 'do you see Great Bear?'

Eko nodded wearily.

'See how it move since last I show you?'

And indeed it had moved, the handle of the great adze in the sky, had spun almost a quarter the way round, since first they had spied it. It would move the same again before they had done.

'When the handle come due west, the stars will fade. It will be near dawn. The end of all this.'

Jeuy was doing his best to keep Eko amused. Apart from the glorious stars above them, there was very little to see in the desert gloom. All was just endless road, the backs of the pack animals. Eko tried his best to play along.

'Where' he said, 'is Osiris the hunter?'

Jeuy thought for a moment, scanning the sky. Orion, the star of Osiris, was nowhere to be seen.

'Well you see' Jeuy replied, 'at this time of year, Orion is in his underworld. Isis too, searching as she does. You not see either again for another month. Isis will return first, with Ra, at the final gate of night, just before dawn.'

'What do you mean?'

'The Dog-star – the Soul of Isis – she will rise to open the year with Thoth.'

'Oh I want to see that. What's it like?'

'The inundation? Don't tell me you never see that ... oh well, living in Alexandria, it is not the same ... "the tears of

Isis", shed in terrible grief for her murdered brother and lover. Close on the heel of Isis he come, just as Orion return to the night sky. He is late getting dressed. He just manage to get foot in the door, before Ra arrive at the seventh, the final cavern of the underworld. He fling open the gate of dawn. He fill the sky with light, so bright, that all the stars invisible.'

Eko, though exhausted, managed a laugh at the image of Orion, oversleeping, and waking with a start, rushing down to his place, just in time for dawn. It was something to do. Would the first star of Orion make it before it all got too light for him to be seen? When that happened, they must be nearly there, close to the desert crossroads at Phenicon. Near to the end of this interminable night march. Break their fast on the company's bitter porridge. Then a good sleep stretched out next to their things. Eko would soon forget the whole thing, especially the bit about it starting again come sundown.

Eko dozed. When the monotonous pace of the caravan slowed, he reopened his bleary eyes. The sky was a dark mauve.

'Are we there yet?' he grumbled.

Zenobia repeated the question. Everyone was asking something. 'Why is it going so slowly?'

'Why has it stopped?'

Someone nearby, familiar with the journey, called out, 'we are not far but still a mile or two out. This is an auxiliary hydreumata. There will be water, but very little else until we move down the valley, into Phenicon. Why are we stopping here?!'

No movement. The sky grew ever lighter. Someone said it was too late to move on. The camels need to be unloaded. The camels need water. They will become angry. We need to sort ourselves out. We need to eat. It has been a long night. We must rest.

The word went round that they would not be moving into Phenicon. This would be the day's pitch. The disappointment was tangible. Images of the luxuries of Phenicon had driven many on through the long night. Now this primitive camp was it. The sharing of whatever rations could be had. And what would tomorrow bring?

A delay in Phenicon was a mixed blessing. Would the headman allow the extra day on the journey? The loss of his bonus? Likely he would move quickly on through the 'delights' of the desert entrepot.

In the cool of the morning twilight, Zenobia quickly put aside her own disappointment, by organising everyone else. 'Eko' she said, 'are you happy to settle down here and look after the baggage!'

'Oh no' Eko whinged, 'do I have to? I'm not at all tired.'

'I'm staying here if he wants to go play?'

It was the Roman widow. She had attached herself to their little party, as old folk do.

'I'll look after everything.' she preened.

Zenobia looked into the woman's wrinkled face, asking herself whether she could be trusted. She shrugged, her way of saying yes.

'Well if you are sure?'

The widow nodded and smiled at the same time.

'OK, only if you promise you will not go far, just to see what you can find out, about what is happening up ahead.'

Turning to Jeuy, she pointed to the low scrub of the wadi 'do you think there is anything to eat out there?'

Jeuy shrugged.

'Maybe, berries or rabbit.'

'Ok – let us go' she obviously meant to join him, but a hundred yards out, he indicated that they should fan out into the scrub. 'You go there' he said, pointing to a clump of acacia scrub, 'I look by the rock.'

She looked at the bushes – perhaps it was the wrong time of year – there was nothing edible to be seen. She found herself working in a small semicircle towards Jeuy's 'pitch'. She did not call out. Unconsciously she was very quiet. He was nowhere to be seen. Perhaps Jeuy was already back at the campsite. Her eye fell on his turbaned head, just visible above some desert thorn. She saw he'd removed his desert shirt, and was busily engaged in his morning ritual, carefully cleansing his perfect skin. Zenobia allowed herself a guilty pause before subtly making him aware of her approach. Again she allowed herself to be surprised at just how well muscled and smooth was Juey's body. She coughed. Which might in other circumstances have made him call out nervously, *who's there*? This time, he simply turned a little toward the sound, at the same time knowingly retrieving his julabia from its hanging place on a nearby branch. Zenobia caught the tiniest hint of his belly, the woolly, wolf-like hair.

'Oh it is you? she giggled awkwardly, 'Any luck?'

'A little' he replied 'I have desert wheat but will take a while to prepare.'

'Better get back.'

'Yes better get back.'

At the camp, cooking fires were consuming the freshness of the morning air. Jeuy dehusked the primitive wheat, ready to parch the grains in the embers of the fire. A long job, unlikely to yield results in time for that day's meal. Zenobia craned her neck, looking for Eko. Where was he? He ought to be back by now.

There was a commotion. A wave of realization rippled down the huddled caravan. The peace shattered by Eko's terrified shouting:

'The Romans are coming! The Romans are coming!'

Eko ran to them. Cunning as a desert fox, he dodged every attempt by first one man, then another, to grab his arm, to make him to explain. In moments he was panting in front of Zenobia, Jeuy and the widow.

'What, what is it?'

Now he was breathless. A little crowd drawn into their circle, desperate to hear the excited child's news.

'I've been to the edge of the camp . . . the road to Phenicon. Agents came out to meet our headman . . . to explain the delay.'

Zenobia's normally placid face took on a worried look:

'Calm down,' she soothed, 'Did you overhear the conversation?'

'Yes.'

'Are you sure you understood?'

'Yes!' Eko said emphatically, 'I'm not as stupid as you think.'

'I never said you were stupid. What was said?'

'Diocletian has troops in all Red Sea ports. A cohort sent down every desert road, with orders that all travellers are to return to Koptos!'

That was devastating news to all that heard.

'Are you really sure?'

'Yes!'

A collective murmur went around the crowd. A shadow passed over Zenobia's heart. A premonition of what was to come.

'So why do you say they are coming now?'

'They said it,' Eko pleaded, 'the Romans are in Phenicon ahead of us. As we looked, there was a dust cloud on the horizon. It must be them. They are coming!'

Hearing this, a taller man hoisted his brother to his shoulders. He stood a good ten feet above the ground, shielding his eyes, as he peered to the south. With a start he saw the cloud and almost simultaneously the call spread like wildfire, the entire ragged length of the caravan. No Roman boot was kicking up that advancing dust cloud, but something far more powerful. Almost too late, the seasoned eyes saw just what that really was, and screamed. Those screams joined a wave of shouts racing at the speed of sound, the entire length of the caravan. The warning passing each to each – 'Kamsin - Storm!'

12   Rage in the desert

The storm. How it blew relentlessly all that day, lashing them with waves of sand. When describing such a storm, language is so much the poor relation of reality. Nothing moved. It was suicide to expose tender flesh to that savage blast. Within minutes every orifice choked with dust. If not suffocated, blindness, from the abrasive impact of millions of tiny sharp particles was but moments away. Keep the head down, keep covered, for hour after hour of suffocating misery, throughout the long hot stifling day. Every breath filtered through cloth. And above it all the deafening, thunderous howling of the demonic wind. The ancient desert god Seth had them in his implacable grip.

'In the Wind of the mind arises the turbulence called I.

PAN'S ROAD

It breaks; down shower the barren thoughts.
All life is choked.
This desert is the Abyss wherein is the Universe.
The stars are but thistles in that waste.
Yet this desert is but one spot accursed in a world of bliss.
Now and again Travellers cross the desert; they come from the great Sea, and to the Great Sea they go.
As they go they spill water; one day they will irrigate the desert till it flower.
see! five footprints of a Camel! VVVVV'

Zenobia huddled alongside her stepson and companion. The words of an ancient prayer run deliriously through her mind: 'be not unaware of us Oh Seth, if you know us, we shall know thee.' Inbetween bouts of sleep, air starved semi-consciousness, the anxious knowledge that somewhere nearby, the Roman cohort was itself waiting for the storm to abate, before continuing on its savage mission. The soldiers soon to appear, forcing all back down the road whence they came, back to Koptos for swift retribution. The Romans were in control again, their reputation going before them. There was little doubt they had some brutal communal punishment planned for the rebellious town and its fleeing citizens.

Jeuy's musky presence was stretched close by, vainly shielding them with his hard and scratchy muscular strength. His hand upon her hip, steadying himself. No word passed between them, all was lost in a savage, never-ending cacophony. Hour followed hour. All then strangely quiet, something inside numbing the sounds. Thinking the storm was passed, Zenobia called out, but none responded, none could hear, all were deafened so by the raging sounds about them.

She pushed a bare forearm out into the wind, pulling back in an instant, flinching at the stinging sand. Nightfall was the only hope; perhaps the change in temperature would tame the heart of the storm. A real monster could rage for days. Come sunset the storm must abate or they could not survive in such an exposed place. The feeble cloth about them would eventually be torn to shreds, exposing them to the might of Seth, they would all surely die, before the Romans could do the job for him.

Eko was suffering. His body clock not quite adjusted to the nocturnal rhythm, sleeping by day, walking or riding by night. Laying the whole day face down under the feeble canopy of their clothes, was at first a novelty but soon a trial. The stuffy heat and shattering noise. He could almost long for the wonderful bleakness of the desert at night. The coldness of the air, but above all the freedom to move! Eko's aching limbs forced him deeper into the zone between waking and sleep. It was then that he heard the unmistakable voice of Madhavi his mother.

'Patience little one, I am coming.'

'Mother! Where are you?'

The power of the storm enveloped him on all sides. His body was unharmed but he could not see more than a few inches in front of his face. Everything else was darkness. Frustrated he called out, 'Mother, where are you? I can't see you!'

'I cannot be seen.' she replied.

'Mother, please let me see you, just for a moment.'

'Try to understand Eko. What you see is not always as it seems. Do you remember the time I took you to see the Indian sadhu, the holy man? Think about it now.'

Months earlier he found Madhavi alone in their house and looking quite sad. His father was not in the house. Somehow Eko contrived to cheer her and they'd gone together to the forum to see what was advertised as a great wonder. At first he thought they would see the seeress Sosipatra and her phenomenal son, Antoninus. He was all the rage having predicted the downfall of all the city's temples. But Madhavi had other ideas. A holy man of her own race had been buried alive and was about to emerge after an impossibly long sojourn, wrapped in his shroud and entombed deep within the earth.

Eko felt so proud as he walked beside his mother. Even veiled she was a vision that turned many a head. Swaying hips that moved in the steady gait of an elephant, the bounty of her breasts that would bend many a lesser woman.

She strode on, through a circle of unlookers to where panicking men were busy dragging their lifeless guru from the ground. Several awkward moments passed as they frantically worked to bring him back to life. His face was deathly pale apart from his lips which were blue, and his nostrils caked in blood. 'He's dead' Eko shrieked in horror, burying his face in the folds of Madhavi's beautiful sari that smelt so of rose water.

Madhavi knelt down beside him, tossing from her face the thick black hair that was shiny with coconut oil.

'No he's not.' she said, 'look again.'

And indeed though the sadhu's wild hair and unkempt beard were full of grave dirt and dust, he was moving. He looked frightful but was still alive, just. His followers quickly hustling their master's stupefied body away.

When Eko looked again, Madhavi was moving off through

the crowds leaving him behind. He began shouting 'Mother!, Mother!' But she did not respond and the crowds closed around her. Again he shouted, as loud as he could.

But then it was Zenobia's voice he heard telling him to calm himself that he was dreaming. After a few moments he came to his senses and remembered where he was.

'I saw Madhavi!' he yelled. But Zenobia could only mouth the words 'later'. But somehow Eko knew that his mother was still alive and had come to tell him so in a dream.

After a bone-grinding age, the terrible gloom became gloomier. Night was approaching. Jeuy's mouth was close to her ear, shouting. 'Zenobia I think it's calming.'

She shifted to call back 'What shall we do?'

Jeuy was silent.

Another hour passed. Eko had slept most of the day curled up like a spoon at her belly. Now he too began to twitch and move. Suddenly he staggered to his feet. Zenobia tried to pull him back.

'No' he said,' it's gone.'

Indeed the wind had dropped, though the air was still thick with impenetrable dust, that would take days to settle.

Zenobia stood and looked across the devastated campsite.

Here and there the bleating of stricken, dying beasts. Ragged bundles that showed no sign of movement and probably never would. The old and the strong had perished. Eko, Jeuy and Zenobia stared, barely able recognise each other. The fine dust devil had come and left them hardly much more than a pile of filthy rags.

She repeated her earlier, unanswered question:

'What shall we do?'

Jeuy looked hopeless, 'we must go back - the Romans, they will not let us through.'

'But Jeuy, we cannot, we must go on, we must stay on the path.'

Eko was listening intently, then he shouted, 'why, why must we stay on the path?'

They ignored him. What does a child know of the dangers all about them. But he insisted 'why', he repeated this time even more emphatically, 'why must we stay on the path?'

'Because, my dear Eko,' Zenobia said, mustering her reserves of good humour, 'forward or backward, there is no other way!'

'But why can't we go round!! If we cannot go forward or back, we must go around.'

'And what good do you think that will do us, the Romans have all the road in front, all the way to Berenice?'

'Wait,' Jeuy interrupted, 'maybe Eko is right. If we head due south, we will find a road back to the Nile, it is due south of Koptos.'

Zenobia made a supreme effort to calm her voice, 'But what about all our property, we cannot possible carry it with us, even if the agent could find it for us now in all this chaos?'

Juey shrugged before replying. 'Our life, it's more important than things. We have what we need.'

Zenobia saw the truth of it, but still she asked, 'how will we do out there?' With a sweep of her arm, she indicated the vast mountainous wilderness. 'We must get to Berenice . . ' her voice trailed off as she realised the futility of it all.

Juey thought for a moment. 'Listen to me,' he said, 'there are small tracks that connect the main desert road. I know it from when I was a young boy. That cleft in the rock, is the entrance to a great wadi that cut across both of the roads. If we follow, we come on the road to Thebes. With care we walk, it will be hard, but at night it's possible. The Nile is close here than when we start.'

'Yes but what makes you think the Romans will not have that road too?'

'Maybe they do. But it take them into Beja territory. I think they deal with Koptos before they start with Beja. It's our only chance.'

'Yes' Eko shouted excitedly, 'and Jeuy is Beja. If we meet they might help.'

'Madness,' was Zenobia's response, 'all of it. How can we ever survive and find our way through open desert to Thebes? And how will we survive?'

'Here,' Jeuy said, pointing at the pathetic heaps all around, 'many did not survive, their misery is our salvation.'

Zenobia made an exclamation half way between sighing and shouting 'the Roman Widow!' And sure enough she wasn't moving. She hadn't been able to shield herself from the murderous blast. Sometime during the day she had suffocated, coughing herself into oblivion as the fine dust forced its way into her nostrils and mouth. No one had heard her distress.

A shock of recognition passed over Eko's young face. He raced off through the shattered caravan, looking for his friend Hephaestus, the Christian eunuch. His body was already cold. Eko's eyes brimmed with tears. Juey came up silently behind him, then seeing the body, he knelt down for a closer look.

'Why is he dead?' Eko blubbed. Juey pointed to a tiny glass vial that lay beside the body. He uttered one word 'suicide'.

'Hephaestus,' Eko spoke out loud, 'wait for us, tonight

we pass through the seven caverns of the underworld, wait and guide us.' Eko half expected to meet the dead man's departed shade somewhere on the night journey.

A little while later, the three travellers slipped away from the remaining survivors of the ravaged caravan. Jeuy had commandeered an abandoned donkey to carry their things. He pulled the little beast to a halt on a small bluff. The three travellers looked down for the last time upon the flickering campfires of the caravanserai. The stars were bright above them, the moon not yet risen. Zenobia was transfixed by the sight of this warm spot of humanity in the distance. She lingered, not wanting to let it go. Eko was excited again, his mind on other things. 'What is the donkey's name?' he said.

Jeuy looked up from his task and replied, 'he has no name – you make him one.'

Eko's eyes swept skywards in thought, 'Barnabbas' he exclaimed, 'Barnabbas is a good name for a beast.' He didn't know why, he just liked the sound of it.

Jeuy told him to look for two stout sticks. Eko obeyed without question, thinking they were for walking. 'Yes, that too, but first we make a gateway.'

'What??'

'You see, think me mad do you. You soon see method is

my madness. Now listen. When I hold two poles like so, one in each hand, you look to star in the sky, north of us? Find Great Bear, then the pointers, follow them, see?'

'The Bull Stake, I see it?'

'Yes, help me line the gate up, so we pass through to the south.'

After some adjustments, the poles were fixed with heaps of stones. Jeuy left them freestanding, and took his place beside Eko. He was looking for a marker star. 'Got it.' he said, ' Zenobia, we are ready!'

She seemed distracted.

'Zenobia, we go now!'

Eko grabbed for one of the sticks. Jeuy stopped him, 'No', he said, 'not yet'. With a little lampblack he drew the head of a jackal on the left-hand sceptre. On the right he drew that of a ram.

'Zenobia!!'

As if from a dream, she looked up and saw the gateway. Instinctively she began to form the words of the ancient book in her mind. So many times had she read the copy in the double 'House of Life' at Koptos.

'The Desert is bright,' she said, 'I give light with what is on me. (Oh Thou) who destroys men, who art filled with the chosen ones of the gods. Breath be given to you, among whom I am. Let there be rays for you, dweller of the Region of Offerings. My Glorious Eye is for you, I have ordered their destruction, destruction is for all of them. I have hidden you from those upon earth, you to whom the diadem is restored in the Desert. . .'

And with that she led the donkey through the improvised gateway, followed soon after by Eko and Jeuy. Glancing back at her compnaions she gave a weak smile and said: 'let perception be before us and magic steer our ways.'

13   The Seven Caverns

Dropping down. Descending through the wadi entrance, the walls of the canyon rising to their left and right. It was all too obvious that, on those previous days with the caravan, they had made an almost imperceptible rise up to the desert plateau of ancient rock. The wadi cut through the geology, the architechtonic strata that ran all the way down south-westwards towards the Nile valley.

The vast horizon of night sky was now greatly narrowed by steep canyon walls. They must trust to Jeuy's initial calculation to take them in the correct direction. The visible stars offered only limited guidance. After a narrow defile through thick vegetation, things again broadened out, as they entered the first of the 'caverns of the night'. They paused at the rim of the catchment basin of some ancient river, that had once sliced a way through the soft rock in a ghostly rush to the Nile.

'There!' Zenobia whispered in alarm. She pointed to the eastern canyon wall 'I can see a light, up there on the valley wall.'

'Calm yourself,' Jeuy replied in his most soothing voice, 'it's moonrise. A very thin moon, but the lamp of Thoth is a welcome sight in the gloom.'

The silvery point of light detached itself from the cracked rim of the valley top to float slowly upwards into the night sky. As it did so it threw a cadaverous glow over the scrubby, almost imperceptible path, that lay before them.

Juey's anxious expression was illuminated by the pale moonlight. Zenobia wondered why this supposedly welcome sight was now obviously filling Juey with unease? Juey, for his part, had not expected the going to be so dense. At a glance he could tell that the night journey was going to take longer than he'd promised. It now looked as if he had been wildly optimistic if he thought to push a way through this sea of spiky brush. It extended ahead of them. The going was difficult. He doubted they would complete this journey in one night.

Zenobia read his thoughts. She returned an anxious look at Jeuy then Eko, who asked:

'Do you think it will be alright?'

'I don't know,' Jeuy replied, with as much calm as he could muster, ' yes, I think so, Eko my son, you must ride up here on Barnabbas. If we spend the day in the wadi, there is shade, water too, if we find the spring. Food if we look.'

* * *

The seemingly endless sea of thorns revealed by the baleful moonlight, turned out to be far from impenetrable. It was the first of many illusions. The going was tricky but there were gaps between the bushes, the traces of a track. These were the well worn ways of desert creatures, foxes perhaps even a gazelle; nothing bigger, they all hoped. But the way was not the most direct. Several times they followed a false trail that led to a dead end, or took an unexpected trajectory; forcing them to retrace their steps or risk loosing their bearings.

Eko stirred from his perch on the donkey's back.

'Jeuy' he said, 'I'm bored up here. I want to walk.'

'No,' Jeuy replied, placing a hand on Eko's knee, 'best stay there out of the way of the harm. For boredom, I tell a story.'

Eko would rather have walked, but knew it was best not to argue.

'Yes,' he said, 'tell me a story.'

Juey thought for a moment, a weary, knowing glance from Zenobia, the only assistance she would give. Then a look of readiness.

'Do you know the tale of Setna Khemwaset?'

'Of course,' Eko groaned, 'everyone knows that one. My father Philo told it all the time.'

'OK,' Juey said desperately, 'what about his second tale?'

'Is there one?' Eko and Zenobia levelled their most sceptical looks at Jeuy.

'Of course,' he replied, although the wry look on his face made Eko suspicious.

'There isn't! you're just making this up?'

Zenobia smiled.

'Ah, whadoyouknow,' Juey crooned triumphantly, 'there are many tales of Khemwaset, the famous magician,'

'Magician!' Eko interrupted, 'Isn't that a word the Romans use whenever they disapprove of the Egyptian priests!'

'Maybe,' Jeuy reposted, 'you are right, in our tongue, magician is a Heka, and magick Hekau. But don't interrupt or you spoil my story. It is good one.' He cleared his throat.

'The second tale of Khemwaset. Many years after adventures with ghostly mummies, his quest to find Thoth's legendary, magical book, his repentance, his restitution to rightful owners. Nanofer and Ahuri's reburied together after years of separation. Do you remember all?'

'Yes, yes, yes, yes, I remember it all!' Eko seemed adamant.

'OK, so new story begins years after those things. The fame of Setna Khemwaset spread throughout the land.' Juey's voice rose in a more stentorious tone. 'He is most powerful Heka, loved and respected by the King.'

'Has he married?' Eko interupted.

'He married, to beautiful lady, Mahi.'

'And do they have children?'

'No, no children.'

Juey continued, 'and that was great shame to both. For all Setna's supernatural power, they could not conceive child. Mahi never ceased praying in temple of Ptah, praying he send a child.'

'She should have slept in the temple of Ptah,' Zenobia now interjected. She smiled wryly as she remembered how she had done the same and how it hadn't worked, 'The god would have sent a dream.' she said.

'It's a child they want, not a dream!'

'Silence, both of you,' Jeuy fumed, 'let me tell story. That is what she do. She went to temple.'

'And Ptah sent a child?' Eko again interrupted.

'Almost,' Juey continued, 'the god, he sent instruction for magical potion. Mahi, she drink this, before she and Setna sleep. So, when water of conception pass in the night, she become pregnant?'

'And it worked?' Eko squealed.

'Yes it worked. And that child was Saosiris – brother of Osiris.'

'And now you must go through all the boring bits when the child is growing up?'

'Well yes, one want to grow up quickly. But it happen, Saosiris grew up twice as quick as other child. At school he was better than all classmate. He already knew the lesson. Which,' Jeuy said, pausing for effect, 'is no surprise, because it not first time he was born.'

Zenobia shot him a knowing glance. Eko, now entangled in the lot, had to ask:

'Is that true Jeuy, can someone be born twice?'

Jeuy drew the donkey to a standstill.

'What does Zenobia think?' he asked.

'Me, what do I think?' Zenobia said, clearing her throat, 'Yes, actually I do think we have all been here before and, given the right knowledge, will return again.'

'And not die?'

'A person dies, but the scriptures say a knowing person

returns again and again, as indeed you will find in your story – Saosiris is no doubt some reincarnating magician, probably a mirror image of Setna Khemwaset – this is how these stories always go – wheels within wheels - boxes within boxes.'

'Zenobia – you're telling me the ending!'

'Opps, sorry. I just wanted to say that I think, if we are to return, it will not be by faith in the gods but by our own wits – but Juey finish his story.'

'Yes Jeuy, finish my story!'

Pausing for effect Jeuy continued:

'As you guess. Saosiris was a clever young man. The spitting image of the father.'

'Ho Ho!'

'Yes, ho ho. One day, two funeral processions pass the terrace of the house. One is rich man, the other is poor. Saosiris's father, Setna, sighed when he saw poor man. Before he knew he say aloud, "May I be received in the realm of the dead like rich man." But then son made reply that astonished his father: "I would sooner you left world as poor man than rich one!" he said.

"But how so," Setna said, "do you despise me so much?"

"No father, if you let me show you how each of these people fare, poor man who goes to death unmourned. Rich man buried with much honour, I think you not doubt my love."

"How can you do such a things?"

'Saosiris uttered enchantments, unknown to Setna.' At which point Juey took a deep breath and began to moan, as if chanting some terrible word of power EEEEEEE,'

'Yes Jeuy,' Zenobia said smiling, 'we can do without the theatrics!'

Juey stopped moaning and continued, 'Saosiris took father by the hand. He lead him to mountains of Memphis. They passed two high cliffs of rock into great cavernous valley. It was first of seven caverns of night.'

Eko was no longer laughing. Something in the tale unnerved him. The turn the story had taken scared him.

'Like us now,' he cried, 'we are in the caverns of the night? We will see a ghost!'

'This is no cavern!' Jeuy pleaded

Zenobia's eye was upon him, burning a hole.

'Better stop now,' he said, 'Eko, you rest. I finish story tomorrow, in the light.' After that they walked in silence for a long while.

The goddesses of the hours toiled. The stars changed position. The moon that had risen on the eastern wall of the canyon, made its way across the sky and was close to setting, leaving the heavens the deep mauve colour that heralded the approach of another sunrise. The last few decans of stars were making their way over the eastern horizon, struggling to be seen before the steadily lightening sky burnt them away.

Eko was as much asleep as the awkward gait of the donkey beneath him would allow. Jeuy and Zenobia looked at the lightening sky, then at each other. They both saw each other's anxiety beneath the fatigue. They knew that their hope of making it though the wadi during the night were forlorn. The soaring heat would soon compel them to find a shady place to camp during the hottest part of the day. The journey must start again at nightfall.

'Here' Juey pointed.

Zenobia followed his finger 'What is it?'

'Caves. Up on right. They are deserted. We shelter or if is anyone there, ask for shelter.'

At that moment, the faint unmistakable sound of singing drifted down from the rocky bluff above them. Exchanging knowing glances, Jeuy and Zenobia spoke as one: 'Jacobites!'. The strange word jolted Eko from his stupour: 'A wish, a wish!' he said. They smiled as they remembered the child's game.

'Go on – see if you have a second!!'

Sighing with good-natured resignation, for he was as tired as a dog, Jeuy started the count down:

'Three, two, one . . .'

'Sacred Bast,' Zenobia and he spoke together. Then again:

'Desert camels!'

Eko squealed with delight, 'That's three. Three wishes!!

Juey was too tired to remember the third line and when he said 'Wadjet', Zenobia said 'Amon' and the spell was broken.

'Oh not so bad' she said, 'three is better than one. Eko what will your first wish be?'

He thought for a moment, then replied:

'I wish, I wish, that whoever is singing is a friendly person.'

'Indeed, let it be.' Jeuy said, geeing the donkey up via a narrow track, that seemed to promise egress to the bluff, just below the caves.

The singing came from within. They heard the unmistakable 'Kyrie Eleison' of the Jacobite liturgy. Had it just begun? If so then they might have a long wait before they could make their presence known, and ask permission to stay. Several minutes crawled by. They sat. Several more minutes elapsed. They drifted into a light doze, from which they were roused by an imperious voice: 'What do you want?'

A long skeletal streak of a man was speaking; his greying beard grown down to his chest, his skin, tanned by the desert sun, was pierced by the most intense blue eyes. Most distinctive of all was the still unmistakably red hair – a feature not so uncommon in upper Egypt, where such people were once known as Sethians. As was Jacobite custom, he leant on a Tau-shaped crutch, although he was not lame. Though his clothes were simple, his presence was imposing. Eko's young brain was the first to retrieve its wits, responded:

'Papa, we travellers beg permission to camp for the day, to let our beast forage a little for food.'

14   The Hermit's Lair

The hermit turned his back and strode away almost as quickly as he had arrived. His only response, a grunted: 'Huh!'

Eko, unaware of the laws of the desert, was confused, which left Juey to scuttle after the anchorite, pleading 'Papa, may we share food with you, we not have much; this desert wheat, collected yesterday, will it not make fine bread?'

Juey knew that the Jacobites were strict vegetarians, subsisting on a diet chiefly of lentils dressed with olive oil, perhaps an onion washed down with water, or beer made from the fermented fruits of the nettle tree, but never wine.

At last the hermit turned. The sour look now replaced by one of pleasure. Though at the time they did not know it, he declaimed a line from one of his holy books:

'He may be known by his hospitality to strangers and be praised for his fruit.'

Hearing this, Juey asked that they have the use one of the caves. This evinced another grunt, following by a brief sweep of the holy man's arm, which said, *take your pick, they are all empty, and free.* Juey made the sign of silence to Zenobia, quickly hustling her towards the cave. He feared the parting shot of the anchorite might be: 'No women!'

Zenobia scuttled out of sight through the low door into the cave, just in time to hear the Papa shout, 'Do you want water? There is water, just in that gully up there!'

'Thank you Papa,' then on an afterthought, Juey called back 'How shall we know you? What is your name?'

The holy man hesitated, as if trying to remember, then shouted 'Hadra!' Had he forgotten his own name? Here in the lonely desert, it was not such an unusual thing.

With that, he strode off towards some unknown errand.

'Water?' Eko's question made Juey turn.

'Can there be water here in the desert?'

'Yes my Eko, it happen, we are blessed, you have your wish. Go to Zenobia, I graze the beast,' then correcting himself, repeated 'tend to friend Barnabas. I soon come.'

The rock-hewn cell of yellowish earth was very small,

poorly furnished, without timber, plaster, order or symmetry. The crude cave ceiling was so low, even Eko could reach up to touch the pale rock with his hand. A tall man like Hadra, could not have stretched to his full height in such a room. What little light there was entered through the cave door. When closed, light streamed through a small bladder-shaped grill of holes bored through the wall.

'How do they live here?' Eko asked

As always, Zenobia had an answer: 'Their rule obliges them to renounce matrimony for ever, to renounce all carnal desires, never to see their parents, to possess no estate, to dwell in the wilderness, to be clothed in wool, to be girt with a leathern girdle, to eat no flesh, nor drink wine all their lifetime, to shorten their dinner and to deny themselves all the nourishments without which the body is able to live. It commands them to employ all their time in fasting, prayer and worship, to have always their mind running upon their God, to apply themselves to the reading of Holy books and to understand the truths that are there contained.'

'Phew,' Eko interjected, 'you know a lot about them.

Zenobia replied with her habitual shrug.

'What of sleeping?' Eko asked, 'there is no bed roll on the ground?'

Zenobia yawning heavily before replying, 'I am sure the

previous occupant took away his sheepskin from the very spot in which we shall now lay ours down.'

'Here' she said, 'let us make a place for Jeuy, ready for his return. We shall all sleep a while. Come lie down here, beside me and sleep.'

Eko needed little encouragement to do that. Though dog-tired, he could not stop the endless questioning of his mind.

'Zenobia,' he said sleepily, 'does the holy men's rule oblige them to sleep upon a mat on the ground, never to sleep on a bed?'

'I have heard,' she replied, her voice becoming thick with sleep, 'they may have a bed only if their superior thinks they are sick. Even then, they must not take off their clothes, or their girdle, never sleep two upon the same pillow as we are now, nor even near one another.'

Eko's voice was now heavy with weariness. But he still had one further question: 'what do they do here?'

'Their rule obliges them to pray,' she said, her words punctuated by unsurpressed yawns, 'to prostrate themselves, one hundred and fifty times before they go to bed, their faces and bellies to the ground, to spread out their arms in a cross, the fists shut tight. At every rising, to make the sign of the cross, which renders them very lean, and cast down, so they appear like so many skeletons, rather than as men.'

They fell asleep at the same instant not even noticing Juey's return.

The prehistoric calls of roosting desert birds brought Zenobia back to her senses. She opened an eye in time for it to fall upon a tiny gecko stalking some unseen insect across the cave ceiling. Other than her reptilian friend, she was alone. The quality of the light told her it was twilight. Her feet and legs ached. She lingered a little among the familiar smells of her bedroll, willing herself to rise, join the others, who would no doubt be preparing to leave, for it was already late in the day. Her tired body felt so heavy it was as if it would sink through the sheepskin into the earth beneath. Only with great effort of will would she be able to pull herself to her feet.

A few moments more, she thought, then up. 'Uppp' but as she did so Eko came in: 'Wait Zenobia, no need for rush. Hadra, the Holy man, is in no hurry for us to go. Jeuy thinks it may be a good thing to stay one night, and move on again the next day evening. Yes?' he said imploringly, but nevertheless confident in his ability to weedle Zenobia, although knowing that it was really her call. If she insisted they move, then they would move.

She sank back on the sheepskin. Eko, taking that as a yes, immediately disappeared again, out through the cave entrance, gabbling excitedly to himself.

'I think the old man has been long in the desert. He not recognise a woman, unless you say it.' It was Jeuy speaking now, his words rousing Zenobia from her abstraction, 'Keep covered, say little, I think it be all right. Beside,' Juey continued excitedly, 'he is preparing food. When sun go down, we join him, he say prayer, read from holy book, not too long, we eat, do lots of talk, he want gossip.'

Eko rushed in 'Zenobia, say yes, please.'

Zenobia paused before replying, weighing the options. 'Yes, let's do it'

'Whoopeee!'

A worried look came to her face as she reminded them both: 'the Romans are still close by, perhaps this Hadra has advice on the way ahead. '

'Jeuy, is that water good?' she pointed to a simple earthenware jug, stoppered with a crude cup of the same material.

'Yes, it's good, I changed it when you sleep. There's a spring in the gully, monks make good use, growing vegetable, on terrace hewn from the cliff. They live good here.'

Zenobia drained the cup. 'More,' she pleaded, and when she'd drunk that, she asked whether there was a place to wash up in the spring.

'Yes, it's a paradise here.'

They three were dawdling over their ablutions when the the clank of an iron bell sounded from the hermitage. The metal sound evoked the seven runged, iron ladder of Seth and Horus, on which Osiris ascended to the skies. Only now it must be Jacob's Ladder.

It was time to join Hadra, who'd been busy preparing the simple desert chapel. The bell was a summons to join him in the antechamber for the evening offices.

When they got there, Hadra was in the main shrine, shielded by a ragged but still beautiful veil, through which the light of several oil lamps cast an ethereal glow. The smell of burning olive oil mixed with incense, filled the cave temple. From the familiar chants of 'Kyrie Eleison', less familiar, mumbled prayers, reached their ears and stifled the occasion groan of an empty stomach. They three companions exchanged longing looks.

Eko's pained glance to Zenobia said:

'How much longer, I'm starving.'

To which Zenobia replied with an equality parsimonious

gesture, a mere shake of the head that indicated a need for patience. In truth, she too was ravenous.

Finally, after an age, Hadra emerged from behind the veil, clutching a small codex, that looked to be bound in gazelle skin, probably the same beast whose skin provided the parchment for the contents. Only the most valuable or precious books were prepared this way. Zenobia mused on how Hadra's undoubted 'sethian' ancestors would turn in their graves at this use of the gazelle, which like the pig or goat were the enemies of Osiris. Parchment was a magical paper used in all things, where the old enemy needed to be suppressed by Thoth's art of writing.

Hadra bade them sit, taking his place on a low stool just a head height above them. He placed the precious book on its barque, a shrine of delicately carved desert wood.

Clearing his throat he said 'The Gospel of the Egyptians'. It was the obvious prelude to a reading from the holy book. How much longer, the three pilgrims thought, whilst with all their will they did their damndest to looked interested.

Mercifully, Hadra first passed around a large cup of unfermented grape juice, chased by a freshly baked, divided bread loaf, no doubt prepared from the desert wheat that had been their arrival gift.

The food and drink was a welcome although temporary respite from their hunger.

He began to read:

'And he took them with him and led them to the cleansing-place and walked into the temple. And there came near a Pharisee, an high priest, Levi by name, and met them and said unto the Saviour: Who hath given thee leave to tread this holy place and to look upon these holy vessels, without thy first bathing thyself, and without thy disciples having washed their feet, but unclean *as thou art,* hast thou walked in this Temple, which is a clean place, wherein no man walkest but one that hath bathed himself and changed his clothes, not presumeth to look upon these holy vessels?

And straightway the Saviour stood with his disciples and answered him: Art thou then clean, that art here in the Temple?

He said unto him: I am clean, for I have bathed myself in the pool of David, and when I have gone down *into it* by the one ladder, I came up by the other: and I have put on white and clean raiment, and then did I come, and have looked upon these holy vessels.

The Saviour answered him and said: Woe unto you, ye blind, that see not! Thou hast bathed thyself in these waters that are poured forth, and into night and day, dogs and swine are cast, and after thou hast washed thyself didnst scour thine outer skin, which the harlots also and flute-girls anoint and bathe and scour and beautify to arouse desire in men, but within it is filled with scorpions and all evil. But I and my disciples, of whom thou sayest, that we are not washed, have been washed in living waters that came down from God. But woe unto them that wash the outside but inside are unclean.'

Hadra stopped reading and looked at them. Zenobia wasn't sure if he saw understanding in their purposely blank faces, although the passage had an obvious, if radical message, convincing her even more that the monk must be a Sethian. Hadra looked quickly from Juey to Zenobia, his fingers finding another passage:

'Salome saith:'

Eko almost choked with laughter, hiccoughing instead. For Salome was a very common name in Alexandria. Hadra gave the merest blink then continued: 'Salome saith, until when shall men continue to die?

Now the Scripture speaks of man in two senses, the one that is seen, and the soul: and again, of him that is in a state of salvation, and him that is not: and sin is called the death of the soul

It is advisedly that the Lord makes answer: so long as women bear *children*.

To which Salome replied 'I have done well then, in not bearing *children?*'

As if childbearing were not the right thing to accept.

The Lord answers and says: 'Every plant eat thou, but that which hath bitterness eat not.'

Salome then inquired when the things concerning which she asked should be known, the Lord said: When ye have trampled on the garment of shame, and when the two become one and the male with the female *is* neither male nor female.'

They were strange words that set Zenobia's mind running in a circle. Her eyes caught those of Juey. He looked confused, as was she. *What was that about*, she wondered, she understood the part about purity being an inner quality. The childless thing, that was odd, maybe it meant that not all offspring need be the product of one's own womb?

Hadra knotty fingers were already smoothing down the page, searching for another passage. One each perhaps: Glancing briefly at Eko, he read:

'Take no thought from morning until evening
nor from evening to morning, either for

>your food, what ye shall eat, nor for your
>raiment which ye shall put on. Much better
>are ye than the lilies which do not card
>nor spin having one garment which suffices,
>who can add unto your stature? His disciples
>say unto him 'When wilt thou be manifest unto us and when shall we see thee.'.
>
>He saith: 'When ye have put off your raiment and are not ashamed.'

Hadra closed the book, returning it to the shrine. There was silence, punctured only when he lifted an oil lantern and with an imperious flick of his head, indicated that they should follow him, out into the cooling night air, to a small encampment. There they hoped to find their supper, and perhaps talk a little about the strange holy man's even stranger beliefs, if only out of politeness. They were not disappointed.

There was cool water to drink, pure or mixed with Hibiscus. Olive oil in which to dip more of that unleavened bread baked with the desert wheat. A large bowl filled with fresh lettuces, two each, their sap still bitter and overlaying the strains of the day with easy euphoria. Lentil soup, Ful beans, a basket of nuts, and fresh dates – a veritable feast after the privations of the journey thus far. Such was their mutual hunger they ate in silence.

Only when hunger was defeated, did Hadra lean back from the food to speak. 'I would say, I pray you, "how fares the human race; if new roofs be risen in the ancient cities: whose empire is it that now sways the world?"'

Zenobia wondered if Hadra always spoke with the words of others. Juey snorted, which caused Hadra to turn a questioning eye upon him.

'Juey means no offence.' Zenobia intervened, her clear voice perhaps breaking the unspoken assumption that, as a woman, she should be seen but not heard.

Eko, seeing the mistake spoke in order to mask Zenobia, 'Yes father, in the world outside bad things happen, roofs are pulled off houses.'

'Yes indeed, it cannot have escaped your notice that we too,' the sweep of his hand indicating the empty cells of the desert monastery, 'we too, are in crisis.'

But Zenobia meant to assert her role as *de facto* leader of their party, dropping the pretence she spoke directly to Hadra: 'what has happened here?'

Hadra sighed heavily before replying, 'Everyone has fled,' he said, raising a hand in the familiar gesture of exasperation, 'gone back to their villages or to other communities, south of here - many to Ombos.'

'Ombos?' Zenobia countered, 'Ombos, the golden? The deserted city, or so I have heard, deserted for centuries.'

Ombos, the city of gold, or Nubt in the native tongue, was on the western bank of the Nile. The priests in Koptos said it was one of the oldest cities in the world, founded by the dark lord Seth, but long abandoned, and visited only by those wishing to lay offerings in the crumbling precincts of the god's ancient citadel.

Zenobia wondered whether the Jacobites, with their affection for deserted places, had founded a new colony in the ruins of the ancient metropolis. How fitting, she thought, given Hadra's red hair and sethian looks. Was the Jacobite god a form of Seth?

'Indeed my dear, Ombos is an abandoned city, but that is how we like it. There, in the foothills, is a new monastery, dedicated to the three unknown saints, where you will find those that were once here. For as you know, the Romans are returning to the eastern desert. Those of our religion are particularly unwelcome in these parts. Naturally they fear they will wake one morning to find their heels pierced with chains, marching to a grisly fate in a Palestinian mine.'

The last phrase struck the three travellers dumb with fear.

It was Eko who broke the silence – speaking rapidly and nervously: 'we too are escaping Koptos – we were part of a caravan heading for Berenice, but the road at Laquetta was blocked by a Roman cohort. We left the road.'

'Well you did well, word is the Romans mean to push the stopper into Koptos. An evil fate awaits the citizenship for their support of the rebellion. You did well to get off the road when you did!'

They seemed brighter at the news: 'do you think we shall make it back to the Nile?'

Hadra's brow creased as he said: 'If you are quick – the Roman gaze is focussed now on Koptos. The other roads south, are still in the hands of the Beja. The Romans fear them, and will be anxious to make a treaty. One way or another, their attention is turned to Koptos. But when they are done, who knows what they will do?'

'What then indeed?' Zenobia said under her breath.

'My advice to you is stay clear of all the cities on the Nile so close to Koptos.' Hadra paused, clearly weighing all the options. 'You could do worse than to go to Ombos. I'm told there are abandoned houses all around the monastery. The monks may not take you in, but they are required to assist you with food and water. If you choose this route, I may be able to contrive an errand for you, that will do as an introduction.'

Zenobia was ahead of him, she had already guessed what this might be. The three unknown saints could not remain so indefinitely. To divine and remember their names would require special magick of the kind that needed a young boy medium. 'Suffer the little children to come unto me'.

Feeling himself momentarily the focus of attention, Eko thought he might capitalize on the position, by asking some clever question, about Hadra's compline reading.

'Father – may I ask a question about the reading?'

'You may – did one passage in particular strike you – as it came out, there were three passages, one for yourself, one for your mother and the third for . . .'

'She is not my mother!' Eko snapped with surprising vehemence.

'Peace boy, she is your mother in this place!. . .' It was an awkward moment, rescued by Juey's good nature: 'Eko is in a manner of speaking, a step-son. We last heard of his natural mother in a letter from Alexandria, which he bring, in his journey to safekeeping in Koptos. We've heard nothing since – although she promise to join us as soon as she and …'

'My father,' Eko again interrupted, 'my father can escape the city and come get me.'

Hadra could see from both Eko and Zenobia's faces, that they did not hold too much hope, that either parent would actually arrive. Hadra asked, with as much kindness as he could muster, what was the name of Eko's mother.

'Madavi' came the reply, which only served to increase Hadra's puzzlement.

'Why that look?' Eko said, 'have you heard of her?'

'No, I'm afraid I have not. I was merely puzzled by the name. It is not a name I have ever encountered in these parts. Who was your mother?'

Eko didn't want his eyes would give away his uncertain feelings about his true mother. Was he ashamed? He let his gaze drift down, until it fell upon on a point in the centre of the little fire. Who was his mother, was a tricky question. She loved him, he thought so, but she was just too busy to see him when she wanted to. Her words. She was a famous dancer, always busy. There were servants, they saw more of Eko than she or indeed his father, who was also a busy man. It had never been different – but since coming to Koptos, he had spent more time with Zenobia and Jeuy, than he had ever spent with his real mother. It was very confusing.

'My mother, is not a native of Alexandria, she is from India.' he said

Well yes, Hadra had heard of India, one of the oldest of their churches had taken root in the once legendary Musiris, on India's southern coast. No doubt, those same trade winds, that took St Tomas to those shores, returned with exotic cargoes, women such as Eko's lost mother.

Unable to decode the look that passed over Hadra's face, Eko asked outright, if he had heard any news of his mother? It was a preposterous hope.

'No, my son,' Hadra replied, with as much kindness as he could muster, 'news of that kind is hard to come by. But something tells me, that in Ombos, you might find what you want. There is an oracle, still tolerated by the brethren – why not consult it?'

Zenobia was annoyed by such an obvious ploy to manipulate them into journeying to Ombos. But there again, where else were they to go?

'Father do you really think they will know?'

Hadra shrugged.

Eko, his eyes filled with long repressed tears. He looked pleadingly at Zenobia: 'Zenobia?'

'Hush now Eko, we shall see.'

'You mean, we go to Ombos?'

'We shall see.'

Jeuy cleared his throat with a loud 'Ahem!', obviously a prelude to some new conversational gambit. 'But what of the readings from the holy book. Someone do please to say what they mean? Or if I might offer an explanation, in the manner of my own former occupation as diviner.'

Hadra raised an eyebrow but did not object. In truth he was familiar with Jeuy's oracle book and was far from disinterested in what a professional diviner might make of the Jacobite holy books.

'All of the texts allude to the challenge we are facing. There is a warning that appearances can be deceptive. The second passage spoke to me of motherhood and how it comes in many unexpected forms. The third that a body's material needs may not seem so important in the times to come.'

Jeuy was indeed a skilled diviner and his responses caused Hadra to fall into silent meditation making no further efforts at conversation that night

15 On the road again

On the road again. The moribund religious community, abandoned by all except the foolhardy Hadra, already far behind. Eko's mind is momentarily filled with the image of the phantom Roman army, that had risen from the dust storm, what now seemed like days ago. The mirage had sent the entire caravan into a panic on the Pan's road. The shade of his new friend Hephaestus, now lost, swam in his mind's eye. Now a corpse, rotting in the gravel, poisoned by his own hand, in terror at the mere thought of falling again under the control of the Roman authorities.

Eko sighed at the loss of the hope they had all then held in their hearts, despite the hardships. Hope of the road ahead, the way to Berenice and what lay beyond. There to meet one of those monstrous ships in whose belly or if they were fortunate enough, on whose deck, they would spend forty days and forty nights at sea. They would be exposed to the elements unless money allowed for the extra comfort of a rough shelter. The monsoon winds known as 'Hippalos' would drive their ship out of sight of the land until it reached legendary Musiris in the extreme south of India. This was the birthplace of his real mother, Madhavi. Eko hoped against hope that she would be waiting for him there.

All seemed impossible now. In the middle of all that, a dream of dismemberment – was it Eko on the block or someone else. He was observing all, from high up in the corner of the room, where his discarnate spirit, his Ka, hovered expectantly. He saw the flesh, all blues, greys and purples, wobbling aside before the over-sharp knife, as it sliced its way through the body's midsection. The thought of it made him retch.

Seth had sent the dream, it was, after all, his ancient metropolis, for which they were now bound. But the brutality of it – as visceral as any punishment devised in the Roman mind – even those reserved for the worst of their enemies – the kind that struck so much terror into the monks, driving them into exile – visions of prisoners seen and duly noted – noses amputated, teeth gone, ears ripped, heals pierced by greasy chains, making the long march even more unspeakable, as they shuffle towards their hideous fate in Palestine?

Could anything be worse than the Romans, even Seth, whose ancient followers dismembered their dead, circling them under a threadbare tent for a final feast, during which those that remain chew upon the chest bones of the departed, until they felt the spirits return to the ancestral pond.

In his revelry, the circle of ghouls, becomes his fellow students at the expensive Alexandrian academy, to which Madhavi, his mother, finding herself too busy for motherhood, had consigned him. Spit – the topic of this particular day's remembered lesson. Or, if you like, cosmology – the primary substance. By way of contrast, with Greek rationalism, his tutor cannot resist the urge to digress upon the stranger views, of the ancient people of Khem, those who speak of 'spit' as the first matter, or is it semen, similar, similar.

The folk tales speak of those seven sages – did they like lusty workmen, spit into their hands, before straining to raise the remnants of the first Atlantean creation, from beneath the mother ocean, into which it had collapsed? Or was it Amun, wanking into his own hand, the hand of god, the first generation? Beware the spitting magick in these lands. Even the most humble of the *mystoi* cannot do without his or her spit magick.

During this diatribe the pedagogue had risen from his seat. His habitual stoop disappeared as he stretched to his full height, for a moment revealing the remnants of his younger self. The teacher is seeing the face of the young man he once was, before he was metamorphosed into a poet. Was it magic that had done this?

The instant is enough for one of Hadra's many stories to resurface in Eko's mind – sleepily, his head is in Zenobia's lap – the occasional interesting titbit lifting him from sleep. Did Hadra really say, that his prophet once cured blindness by mixing his own spit with the red earth, to form cake like poultices for the victim's eye? And did Zenobia boldly offer her 'histeriola', the *precedent,* that causes such a spell to work, – that Seth, the god of the red earth, blinds his brother Horus, but his mundane sight is miraculously restored by the physician Thoth, the god born of Seth's spit. Each story merges with another.

Eko is back at the Academy; he misses it now, despite that at the time it seemed such an outrage to his dignity. Mother's attempt to be rid of him, so as not to come between her and father's brilliant career. Frequent escapes to the lovely place overlooking the sea made all salty by Seth's spit. The pedagogue did not dare beat him as punishment – he sat with the clever boys, despite his friends being the others, the outsiders – his natural brothers – amongst whom, were several boys, dazzled by his good looks, inherited from his exotic mother Madhavi, felt compelled to protect him from the bigger, rougher boys.

He took them to his special places, threading their ways on snaky paths, lined by a salt encrusted wicket fence, picking their way over the cliff to the beach. His, the awkward responsibility, so he thought, too resentful to do well at the academy. Were his parents ridding themselves of someone, who was absorbing too much of their precious time, time they wanted for each other, and their work?

But all this nodding, sometimes self-pitying fugue, was suddenly punctuated by another primary substance, as Barnabbas, the donkey beneath him, issued the most stupendous fart. That certainly woke him, and after a look shared between the three travellers, otherwise silently plodding their way towards the Nile, the silence broke, and they laughed like satyrs.

How could they know that the grinning teeth of a small Roman patrol, shared their laughter, jeering in rough Greek, at the sight of the rangy Hadra, as he rushed out to greet them? The holy man suddenly reminded of the part of himself he had come to forget, as stiff leather sandals, army issue, connected with his sleeping groin, sending the contents of his food basket, spinning across the gravel, his moans rising higher and higher, as more kicks, punches and blows, rained hard upon him, from the sweaty but brainless mercenaries.

Meanwhile, several miles of safe distance away, Eko, Zenobia and Juey, felt their spirits lifted by the ridiculously flatulent donkey. Somehow in all that mirth, thought of Hadra arose unbid into their minds, perhaps it was the mention of his onion beds, or the beans that had found their way into Barnabbas's feed. There was a slight rise in the path, as it wound a way over a particularly pugnacious rocky outcrop. Here they chanced upon an opportunity to take one last look back towards the hermitage. To their horror, they saw a clear red glow, rising in the direction of the previous night's encampment.

'It's on fire!' Eko shouted. Could Eko's vision be trusted? Juey and Zenobia exchanged anxious looks. Somehow they just knew something bad had happened and that the most likely culprit were marauding Romans, who must have learnt of the hermitage just a day's march from Pan's Road.

Several minutes dragged by.

Juey broke the silence. 'There is nothing we can do, best keep moving.'

Eko wasn't having that.

'We can't just leave him there?' he whined.

'What do you expect us to do?' Zenobia pleaded, at the

same time roughly taking Barnabbas's halter, pulling him forward. They walked on in gloomy silence. All the while seeing images of what might be happening beneath those rising flames. Zenobia vainly tried to quicken their pace, but even she found her eyes scanning the ground, her pace gradually slowing, until they all three came to a dead stop.

'Oh no!' she said. Somehow in the darkness an unspoken decision had been made. They needed to know what was happening. Juey felt it fell to him to return, if that was the consensus. He desire was as great as anyone else's, but he just wished it wasn't him that had to go. He sighed.

'OK', he said, 'you keep moving. I go back, see what I can see.'

But Eko cut him short asking: 'Why can't we all go?'

'How can we all go?' She replied, her voice plainly exasperated, 'Of course we cannot all go,' she paused, 'I will go.'

'What?' Juey spoke trying hard to suppress the relief in his voice, 'Dearest Zenobia, how you go, it is job for a man?'

'Juey, you are my friend. But if you do not mind me saying, you are not the most masculine of men, and neither am I the most feminine of women. If someone must go, I see no reason why not I? In this I have a feeling, Isis is with me in this, do you feel so protected?

'No', Juey agreed, 'he did not. Maybe even Zenobia, 'great in magick', might be out of her depth? You must call on stronger force?'

'Are you asking me to call upon the murderer of my goddess's husband?'

Eko intervened, 'Zenobia, promise, if you go, you will call up whatever power you need, if you are in danger!'

Zenobia's silence was as much of an answer as they could hope for. Again she turned to Juey.

'Eko is our responsibility now, you are my friend, if I go, you must look after him, and get him back to his mother.'

As she spoke, Zenobia moved closer to Eko, heartbroken to see him so emotional. It was a terrible dilemma. She reached out a reassuring arm, that became a tentative pat on his shoulder. She was uncertain whether she would see him again. She wanted to show him she cared, however much he struggled to accept her warmth or resist being passified.

'Nooo!' Eko cried, twisting his narrow shoulders from under her touch.

'Yes, I insist, just keep walking, I will catch up if I can.'

'Noo!' Eko again cried, they were all crying now.

'Zenobia,' Juey blubbed, 'if you must go, we wait here for you.'

She could not argue. She unslung one of her bags and

handed it to Juey. It contained all of her portable wealth. Apart from one other bag, and a small skin of water, she was leaving most of her possessions with man and boy. She embraced them both. They did not want to release her. It was Zenobia who eased herself free. With hardly a hesitation, she strode off into the darkness, in the direction of the beacon of flame.

> # 16 The Cobra's nest

Three of them. Zenobia guessed that of the three, the shorter was the legionaire. To her eyes, he looked typically Roman. With him, two enormous, pale-skinned companions, probably auxillaries from Rome's northern frontier, where men were said to be brainless fighters, addicted to battle. Zenobia picked and crept her way perilously close to their encampment. She did not dare leave the cover of the thorny scrub, that in the gloom, had inflicted several lacerations on her sensitive skin. Though their voices were loud and coarse, Zenobia's hiding place was just out of clear earshot. Neither could she see them clearly.

She heard the voice of the legionaire, barking something, that from the tone, she rightly surmised to be an order to check on the prisoner. Her heart skipped a beat, as he came perilously close to her hiding place, then wheeled off behind a wattle screen, where he looked down on some unseen and prone captive, undoubtedly Hadra.

'Hadra is not dead,' Zenobia thought to herself, voicing internally what she had felt his fate might well have been. If he had been dead, she could have waited for an appropriate moment, silent, sad in the darkness before moving off to rejoin Eko and Jeuy. For a moment an image of them, their faces full of pleasure and relief, swam into her mind. She took this as a premonition, a prodromata for the success of her mission. It filled her with confidence.

I am between the 'altar and the knife', she thought to herself. It was a difficult dilemma – what to do? Why was this Roman patrol, lingering still in what must be a mean and obviously deserted dwelling place? Were they hoping someone else would come? Perhaps they were resting from their march; there was still plenty of time, for such strong men to hurry their way back to the main road, to find their column or to catch it up. Perhaps they were in no hurry to return, with so little to show for their efforts – just one aging Christian priest.

She could hear the legionnaire shuffling about, then something that might be a pitiful groan. Must be Hadra, she thought to herself. Then a rougher shuffle that evinced a loud cry – yes it was Hadra. This was followed by the rough Greek of the mercenary – 'aqua'. Again just groans in reply, followed by the sound of splashing water. In her mind's eye Zenobia could see a rough attempt to give Hadra some water, ending in a ladle full of the precious fluid being dashed into his face.

The sound of it heightened her own thirst – amongst the fold of her dress was a small gourd of water, she licked her lips at the thought of it, but dare not stir to quench her own thirst.

The soldiers called back and forth to each other, indifferently confirming that Hadra was still alive. Zenobia guessed he had received a severe beating. Instinctively she prayed to the goddess, to Isis, to protect him, her, them, but what then? If the soldiers left, she guessed they were unlikely to leave Hadra alive. Zenobia knew she would need very strong forces indeed to rescue him.

The soldiers were back together now, rudely sharing a joke at Hadra's expense. Zenobia shifted slightly to ease the cramp in her hip. Suddenly she felt something that made her heart leap to her mouth. She was not alone in her hiding place! Her hand touched a creature with an unmistakably reptilian feel. Something was there, concealed by the bush's penumbra. In rising panic she realised, she had inadvertently chosen to share her hideout with a cobra's nest. The occupants, too cold to move, were biding their time, waiting until the morning sun warmed their reptilian bodies back to deadly activity!

The soldiers were suddenly on their feet again, busying themselves with their kit. They were preparing to go. The whole scenario flashed before Zenobia's eyes, how at any minute one would break off, cross to Hadra, to finish him, to kill him. How could she be so near and just let it happen, let them dispatch him without a word. But what could she do, she was just a woman?

Then it started, sure enough, one of the big warriors, the same one who had just given Hadra water, was returning, this time his short lethal weapon drawn and ready. It was now or never.

The words of a magical invocation for times of extreme distress were rolling over and over in Zenobia's mind 'be not unaware of me Isis . . . if you know me, I shall know thee . . . arise in peace oh sleeping goddess in the form of Wadjet, the serpent . . . and protect those, that thy faithful servant holds dear in her heart.'

At that same moment Zenobia reached down into the darkness and scooped up one of the sluggish serpents, one hand cupping its fat belly, the other finding the head, as she moved forward out of the gloom, holding the creature in front of her and muttering the most terrifying words she could call to mind.

The soldier was dumbfounded, taken completely by surprise, in sudden terror for his own life, he retreated before her, shouting something in his own barbaric native tongue.

Before he could think, his legs were carrying him away, down the path, quickly followed by his brother. Only the captain was hesitating, on the brink of panic, unsure what was going on, what he was seeing. He was torn between following his men, or doing his duty to find out who or what this dark, snake wielding banshee might be about.

Zenobia could sense the twin desires, it was tangible, the desire for flight or fight, duelling for control. Goddess, yes, drive them away. But in an instant the captain's hands had found a rock the size of his fist. With deadly rapidity, he first weighed it in the air, then hurled it with unerring accuracy at Zenobia. It bounced off Zenobia's brow, cutting short her diatribe with a truncated, choking grunt. The stone dashed out her wits.

She crumpled, letting drop the dormant cobra, which lay, seemingly lifeless next to where she herself had fallen. The Captain was calling down the track to his men, 'it's an old witch. I have killed her!!' But they were out of earshot in the gloom.

He came up closer to her rag-like body, roughly seizing her loose hair, forcing back her blood stained face till the moonlight fell upon it. Zenobia was not dead but she was beyond trying to play so. Involuntarily, she was moaning.

'Ah,' he said, 'a pretty one.'

His blood was up now and with some vigour he tore at Zenobia's garments. 'They'll be back' he said out loud. He dragged Zenobia's limp body back towards the embers of the fire, his tunic offering no impediment to his rising manhood. It was a long time since he'd gone through a woman. He was going to have this one, unconscious or not. If those stupid mercenaries came back soon, they could have her too, but as soon as he'd finished the job, he would finish the job, he would kill her, she would share the stupid priest's fate…

Embraced by the warm, red womb of Seth, the pounding pain in her head was something to be observed from a space just behind the eyes, 'not me at all', she murmured. It was a puppet show, like unto those she'd seen every year of her life, at the festivals to celebrate the rising of the blessed Nile river, those where the confederates of Seth and the companions of Horus, wage war to determine the future of the cosmos for the coming year. Fleeting images flickered before her eyes, like a shadow play, fading again to a livid pink, suffused with blood, sensitive to the touch.

Suspended, she felt the presence of Seth, at first as a crackling sound, almost a physical sensation, electricity in the air, the thick neuralgic atmosphere that comes before the summer lightning, the ozone smell. She was standing beside a colossal statue of the god Seth, but dare not look directly at him. She felt his imperious, distant nature. Taller by far than mortals, as tall as a King, how could he share the concerns of the people, as lady Isis does?

Without looking Zenobia knew him, so familiar was his form, in relief his skin is red, but in solid splendour black and gold, like Isis, his recalcitrant bride. The god's head inclines almost imperceptibly in her direction, any more and the baleful stare of the primitive god would convulse her to atoms.

Where did that thought spring from? Isis and Seth were never lovers were they? Well there are many secret goings on amongst the accursed children of Nuit and Geb, surely such a voluptuous god as Seth would hardly remain satisfied with the frigid Nephthys, anymore than Isis would stay with the dickless Osiris. Zenobia flinches as these thoughts arise unbid in her mind, like bubbles in a swamp – this is Seth's work – master of evil sleep.

'What is happening to me?' she murmurs, wondering why this strange dislocation. She has the distinct feeling that if she looks down, she will see her own body. Something tells her not to look – something is happening there – something so unpleasant, it is best not to know – best to just turn away, cross to the otherside, put more distance between them and us – move on and up, away, never come back. The Roman is violating but her mind is still playing tricks, she sees her husband. Yes something horrible is happening down below, down there, where some life still lingers in the remains of her mortal frame. But why, she wonders, is Seth here alone now? She wants her mother, long dead, to fold her in her arms, cupping her to the breast, stroking her hair, driving the pain away. To carry her to the solar bark, carry her over to the field of reeds. Perhaps it is as it ever was, Seth will again take his place in prow of the boat of Ra, whilst reason will guide them on through the seven hours of the night. Is it that or the more unpleasant truth, that Seth is drawn here, as metal is to a lodestone. Wherever there is dissension, he is there, wherever murder, he is there, wherever rape . . .

A wave of irritation sweeps over her – the god shaking his head. No, that is not it at all; not at all. Don't you know that the gods of one generation are the demons of another? Could she be hearing this, was Seth saying that he was not always evil? No – again the reply came back – that is not it either – not it at all – 'I am as I am'. My nature always passionate – blind passion – many times the all-father clenched his hands into fists. I am one of those fists. Rage you must draw upon! Rage I say, and I will be with you, the speed of the gazelle, the mean strength of the hippopotamus, the verve of the bull, the cunning of the desert fox – rage – and when the battle is done, find my sanctuary and learn the truth.

From somewhere deep within Zenobia felt the seven vowels coalescing into a mighty utterance of rage and power. It gathers there, quickening, all the while fermenting, growing, until it convulses her body, willing itself outward, struggling, forcing its way through her vocal chords, until her head falls letting flow a mighty stream of incoherent sound, gushing from her blood stained mouth.

ERRRBETH PAKERBETH

Her slobbering attacker pauses, then lifts himself up from her, to avoid the ear shattering cacophony of sound bellowed forth into his ear. Almost as soon as his body separated from her, a blistering arrow hisses out of the dark, passing directly through his neck, shattering his vocal chords, sending him backwards into convulsions, as it lodges between the vertebrae of his neck.

Out of sight, further up the track, the hunters are now the hunted. The two fleeing auxiliaries are quickly hamstrung, then hacked to pieces by efficient iron blades. The confederates of Seth had seized their moment to attack.

Barely conscious, Zenobia is fascinated by the convulsive gurgling as her attacker chokes out his last moments. The stranger's strong arms hold her momentarily. Cool water is pouring over her face and into her mouth. Consciousness returns momentarily, enough for her to know these warriors are real.

The archer is dressed in an off-white wrap-around jacket with short sleeves held in place with a belt. His legs and head are bare apart from his large circular earrings of copper. He speaks rapidly in an ancient, strangely familiar tongue, not the lingua franca, not Greek. Zenobia recognises it as a dialect of the native Egyptian tongue. The warrior is barking questions back and forth – is the priest still breathing – give him water – cut his bonds.

The vision in one eye rallies, large strong hands, black skin, blacker than that of Juey – the Nubae, the Nubians, the Beja, desert warriors of Seth. A wave of nausea and pain engulfs her, then a terrible tiredness, dragging her downwards into a pool of warm oblivion.

17 Flight to the river

'Homage to thee, O great god, thou Lord of Truth. I have come to thee, my Lord, and I have brought myself hither that I may see thy beauties.' 'I know thee, I know thy name. I know the names of the Two-and-Forty gods who live with thee in this Hall of Maati, who keep ward over those who have done evil, who feed upon their blood on the day when the lives of men are reckoned up in the presence of Osiris. In truth I have come to thee. I have brought Truth to thee. I have destroyed wickedness for thee.'

The Book of the Dead.

Was she dying? Yes maybe she was. Zenobia's mind struggled to free itself from dark treacle, but was defeated after a few moments of consciousness, collapsing back into the stultifying folds of darkness. Sometimes during these brief moments of awareness, she was moving, borne along carefully, but efficiently, by several strong hands. When they stopped, which was often, someone would pour a little water into her mouth or wash her face. This last action a blessed relief, that cleared her mind for several moments, until the all pervasive throbbing pain in her head reasserting itself, forcing her back into the oblivion of unnatural sleep. Whether it was her wound, or some drug mixed with the water, the effect was the same, as the healing womb of Morpheus swallowed her up.

Night time. The stars above, the balmy Egyptian night air on her skin, the gentle movement of water all around, floating, the alarmed geese calling, each to each, the smell of the Nile again in her nostrils. Everything otherwise so silent.

Zenobia found it hard to rid herself of the fancy, that should she open her eyes, there would be Tahuti, on the prow of the boat, or his father Seth, spear poised, ready to ward off Apophis, the demon of non-being.

Is he there, the Ibis headed one, as he was at the beginning, at the moment she separated from her mother, all those years ago, when he used his lance to separate the umbilical cord, the Apophis serpent, so that one became two, and she came forth into existence? Behind her in the boat, Intelligence, not much use now, as she lay in its belly of reeds, alongside Ra, the All-father, Mehen the all-enveloping serpent, his shield from the elements.

The boat inches away from its berth. For a moment Zenobia hears another, unfamiliar human voice? Who is that? Not Jeuy or Eko, fragments of a prayer, dancing in the air around her, to placate Sobek, the crocodile companion of Seth. The stern voice of some village priest, the invisible gestures of his hands, as they make the sign over the waters to avert the evil eye:

> My sister's love is on yonder side,
> The river is between our bodies;
> The waters are mighty at flood-time,
> A crocodile waits in the shallows.
> I enter the water and brave the waves,
> My heart is strong on the deep;
> The crocodile seems like a mouse to me,
> The flood as land to my feet.

The song triggers cells of memory. The old tale of the two brothers – the infested waterway protecting Bata from the rage of his brother Anubis.

The agony in her skull returns like a black tide, the empty vault filled to overflowing, her cup running over, before the pain god has finished pouring, her head unbearably heavy, forcing her to again retreat within, to one small hiding place in the corner, that secret place where she hid long ago in her parent's house. Again she feels safe, can close her eyes. Time passes. Nothingness flowing over her.

In the darkness, she senses the presence of the goddess of Truth. She remembers she must call out the first of forty-two confessions. Her broken head struggles to remember them. She must call it out, those sins before the denial. What are they, those forty-two sins? She cannot possibly remember them all.

She is a child again, in the House of Life; the scribe is drilling them in the list of sins, that must be avoided if their hearts are to remain pure. No matter how hard she tries she cannot remember them all. The scribe stabs a finger into his palm saying that sins are of two kinds – sins against the gods, sins against fellow men, and of the two, sins against fellow men are the most numerous.

Who has not in some degree sinned against someone? Who has not ever known a worthless man? 'I have never defrauded the poor man' she murmurs, 'or done harm to a slave.' But who can say they allowed no man to go hungry, caused no man to suffer, made no man to weep? People say Zenobia is honest and faithful to the scales of Maat, never cheating by so much as a measure of grain. What little land she has is her own, shared with beasts, managed with grace, neither obstructing not drawing too much from the dyke, where fish swim, without fear, for she has never killed any living thing, has she? Never with intent.

'Have I committed evil in the place of truth?' She does not remember acts of abomination, but who has not thought scorn of the god?

'Have I ever done the things that the gods abominate,

filching offerings of the temple, purloining the cakes of the gods, stolen the offerings of the spirits as some she knows have done, netting the sacred geese, or turned away the cattle from their plots. She has not defiled herself in the pure places of the god of her city, nor ever extinguished a flame when it ought to burn.

'I have not repulsed the god in his manifestations. I am pure. I am pure. I am pure. I am pure.' Nothing, nothing, nothing, but the 'pederast', the lover of Horus? He is with her now, and all is lost, she cannot deny that. What will she say when the gods ask their questions?

But then a strange thing happens. She is there in the Hall of Judgement, the assembled gods, the company of heaven, the boat twisting and drifting on its mooring. The gods, they look but are silent – as if the judgement is not for the likes of us – drifting unimpeded – the ancient corpse lying on its side – drifting on the winding waterway. There is no judgement.

'So I'm not dead', she murmurs. Then for an instant, a fragment of Juey's voice, 'Just dreaming'.

Flashbacks of the moment, the moment the Roman pig, reached for a rock, and swung it at her. The sickening thud, scattering her senses in every direction. Memory, not at all, not at all. Of the fall, the brief return, the scratchy feel of a man's body above her, careless of his weight upon her, his rough hands and amidst it all, his stout penis, like an animal, seeking its prey. The will to resist rising up, the agonising screaming, then it all stops. But yes, one last thing she remembers, the voices in the ancient tongue, the private language, seldom used in public, the one reserved for the family home. Who are they, these desert warriors, these confederates of Seth?

Pain so severe it drives her reeling upward to the mast of the ship, from where she looks down on the others. Her body now that of a human headed Jabiru stork, her Soulba – it is true then. With a pang of emotion, she sees the sleeping bodies of Juey and Eko. They are safe with her together.

She calls, but they cannot hear in their sleep. Her attention shifts to the corpse like one, the face covered by bloodstained bandages, the breathing so troubled. 'I think it best to ignore that one' she murmurs to herself, returning her gaze to look more closely at her Jeuy, the worry lines that even sleep cannot quite relax. Eko, his youthful face, marred now by dark shadows. What are they so worried about? Surely the danger is behind them now? What can be the problem? By reason of her soulba's inelegant but functional stork wings – her spirit flutters around at will, and is apparently unnoticed by all. The tenderness of her love for her stepson seems so poignant. Jeuy too has become very dear to her. 'I must stay close to them both, I must know what has made them sad.'

18 Ombos - Citadel of Seth

Dawn, the flower of the Nile, pushes its sexy bud-like head above the horizon, and, after a moment's hesitation, the lotus bursts open, spreading her petals, all prickly and blue lidded still. Then, in the centre, the brightest yellow areola.

Zenobia is warmed by the sun god. The blood races through her clumsy bird wings, so she can rise up into the sky, above the vast Nile flood plain below, the river snaking its way to her left, the massive shield wall of the western escarpment soaring to her right, shadows moving over the pinky red crags, as they catch the first rays.

Down below, beneath the soul bird's delicate body, the foothills merge into the cultivated strip. The path snakes its way ahead to their final destination, a vast and unfamiliar ancient city, rousing itself from sleep. Its name floats to her across the early morning mist – Ombos – the deserted citadel of gold. Its ancient dusty streets, long abandoned, their ghostly inhabitants fallen into dreamy sleep.

Ombos lies on a natural plateau, bisected by an ancient valley cut by some long forgotten torrent. To the north, the plateau reveals the untidy, but unmistakable by its form, as the faint ground plan of a temple. The temple is a long trapezoid, aligned, in the modern style, with its most holy part adjacent to the western lands of the dead.

Zenobia eyes the fuzzy lines of an earlier northerly orientation. What else can this be, but the temple of Seth? Across the gorge, Southtown, with neatly laid streets that, despite Seth's reputation, speak of good government. Ringed around the city, are several enormous, ancient necropoli, some of which merge with the lost city – whose ancestors, being buried so close to the living, undoubtedly share the same dream.

The soul-bird circles back to the north, flying over a new encampment, that has sprung up close to the moribund temple. The early risers are stirring. Almost there, almost there. The gates flung open. At each quarters lies a towered gate, guarding the cardinal points of the foursquare temenos.

Warrior horsemen emerge from the gate, their white tunics shining in the morning sun, their thighs wrapped in patterned trousers of blue, this repeated at the neck and cuffs. Scales of copper to protect their mid-section, hang from their necks by leather thongs. On the horse's peachlike crupper, sits a light hide shield with a copper boss, the same metal repeated at the owner's wrist. Bouncing beside them is an incised copper helmet, decorated with colourful ostrich plumes, complete with ram's horn cheek-guards. Each cavalrymen carries a javelin, a mace and a large belt knife.

'It is true', she thinks, her heart soaring, 'the Romans will be met with force!' Yet more men emerge from the stronghold, these in more irregular uniform, Greek helmets, shields, and bows. They too have javelins, but fewer horses; most rode camels.

A knot of travellers is moving steadily towards the eastern gate. Well-trodden paths from other gates follow the Nile, or cut steeply up the escarpment to find gravelly roads, across the massive ocean of desolation beyond.

Time to return. Zenobia swoops down, perching unnoticed, beside the unsteady bundle, that swings from an improvised palanquin, the ridgepole resting on the strong shoulders of Nubian warriors. For the first time she sees a second palanquin, but where is the daemona, the Ba spirit, none appears, does the occupant sleep?

The end in sight. The caravan quickening its pace. A single unarmed man, racing to meet the scouts from the camp up ahead. They are in the blinding morning sunlight before a low stone tower. Words hastily exchanged, the swinging, parcels moved into the cool gloom of the gatehouse, there to be gently lowered to the stone flags. Urgent words ring out in the ancient mother tongue.

'Bring them into the shrine - hurry!'

Zenobia's soul-bird alights on an empty wall niche, from where she has a good view of the entire chapel, from the doorway to the holy of holies. With a start she sees the Ka of a stout looking Roman centurion. Is she afraid, no she is no longer afraid. He does not look as mean as the one who had mortally wounded her on Pan's Road. But the incongruity of it all, finding Horus here – complete with javelin, to spear his old adversary.

The air about him is thick with his habitual gesture – first steadying himself with both fists drawn up to the side of his head, then throwing forward first one arm, then the second. Bending over, as if to lift up some very heavy thing, which in an instant, she sees is a leathery Nile monster, a crocodile or hippopotamus. This he lifts on his javelin, raising it up to the ceiling, where it merges with the painted starry pattern.

In a flash she sees the constellation of the Bear, glowing momentarily before becoming one with the other imperishables. Oblivious to her presence, Horus is locked in his eternal struggle with Seth. Does he enjoy the joke? Inbetween each performance, Zenobia sees the image of a white cross over his heart, the lower arm, that of earth, longer than the rest. 'A martyr's death', she murmurs to herself, 'do not ask me how I know such a thing.'

Urgent hissed commands: 'The one who knows is coming, the Sennu, the physician!'

And indeed, a thin looking Beja swept into the room. He sees both patients - going first to Hadra. Zenobia, watching all this, is unsure who is the most infirm, the patient or the doctor, whose own right hand is heavily bandaged. But after a moment, the consultation finishes amid brusk orders for Hadra to be moved.

Zenobia is fascinated, as the doctor moves closer to his other patient, a sick woman on her stretcher. She looks familiar. Jeuy is close, very pale and concerned, as the doctor approaches. Eko too, is biting his lip to hold back tears.

'Please sir,' he says, 'help her, we have money.'

Zenobia cannot hear the doctor's mumbled reply. He gently unwinds her, the bandages, his actions made awkward by his own maimed hand. The wound is exposed. Zenobia peers intently over his shoulder. She sees in the centre of the heavily bruised area, a raised, livid wound, holding still the impression of the missile, with which is was made.

'How pretty' she thinks without thinking. The blow had split the skin into radiating lines forming a neat star-shaped wound. She counts seven points. Though raw, the wound is clean and does not do the weeping that would be a sure sign of an infection. The Sennu continues, gingerly probing the edge of the wound with the finger of his good hand, before laying his entire long palm over her forehead, just above the skin.

'Ah tis good.' he says quietly, almost a whisper.

Juey and Eko speaking in unison, one word: 'What?'

'There is no infection here, the wound is healing well? So why,' he asks himself aloud, 'why does she not wake up?'

He forces open the eyelid of first one eye, then the other. He sighs. He has seen what he needed to see. He replaces the dressing with a clean one, but does nothing more. He prepares to leave, speaking rapidly in Egyptian to one of the others, a youthful assistant. Juey and Eko exchange perplexed looks, they did not understand, but Zenobia does.

Taking the briefest of sideways glances at Juey and Eko,

the doctor says to his assistant soto voice, 'She will not live'. His calm voice continues: 'there is blood behind the bone.'

The assistant asks to be shown how the older man knew this. Without unwrapping the bandage, he shows him the signs. All the time ignoring Juey and Eko, who are becoming distraught. The older man asks the younger if he spoke Greek?

'Yes', he says, 'I know that.'

'Then you better tell them, she may not last the night.'

'Is there nothing you can do?'

'My tongue longs to say yes, but look at me, my hand is still crippled. I do not have the strength for what needs to be done. Tell them.' And with that he left.

Eko spoke first, 'What, what is it; tell us what's wrong?'

'I'm sorry …' , the assistant begins, but before he can finish, Eko and Juey are both sobbing. The youth lowering his head, thinking his job done, makes to leave the shrine. But Juey, with some verve, suddenly leaps across the room, grabbing a handful of the student's coat, shouting:

'There must be something you can do?'

'Ssssh, calm yourself!'

Juey let go, bowing his head, ashamed, muttering: 'I sorry. Is there really no thing you can do?'

The assistant tries to explain:

'Yes, sometimes, but the master here is himself wounded, you saw that, he does not have the strength for the operation.' The assistant hesitates a moment, as if some flicker of hope had entered.

'She may not last the night. But, if she is still alive tomorrow, another doctor will come, an Ursennu, a master, he may help.'

'From where will he come?' Juey pleads.

A tiny flick of the head, a hand gesture, was all that was needed to indicate the red land, the open desert, beyond the northern pylon.

'Then', said Juey, 'I wait for him there to tell him our plight. Eko, you must stay with Zenobia, for her comfort, until I come with the Ursennu.'

The name 'Zenobia' echoes around the room, to the ears of an unseen soul-bird it brings a recognition of its fate.

19 Head loss

She thought dying was not such a bad thing. 'Dying!', she whispered inside her head, 'I am *dying*.' But then, she remembered the desolation on the faces of her companions. Eko, dearest of her heart, his youthful face, should not be that way, such a grim visage. And Juey, him too, she sensed, out near the western gateway, peering anxiously into the gloom; his tanned skin, creased by worry-lines. A mischievous smile formed on Zenobia' face as she wondered whether Juey would break off his vigil to make his morning adoration at the shrine of Narcissus? Would he take his usual meticulous care over his appearance, before coming forth, as the sun god came over the horizon?

Suddenly, she was consumed with a desire to know something of her final resting place, to see her tomb. Zenobia had seen already the ancient necropolis outside the palisade.

I must go there, she thought. In an instant she was up, climbing the thin air, gliding over the ancient city of the dead, spread out across the plain, unlike any she had seen before.

The myriad tombs clustered over tiny damp valleys, cut through the plateau. Strange, she thought, that such locations are the most popular, here, among the dead.

Zenobia's eye followed the lines of tombs as they fanned out, forming thoroughfares, behind which, the less well to do clustered. Strange too, she thought, how the high dry cliffs are almost empty. Did, do, the dead of Ombos shun the cliffs, the gap through which a path wends its way to the western lands, so beloved of Osiris? It was all so perplexing – do not the dead live cheek by jowl with the living. Oh well, she thought, all the more space for her own humble burial.

Swooping down for a closer look, she alighted in the midst of a confusion of tombs, some intrusive on another, or bisected by the corner of a house. Everything is deserted, the silent graves, unbearably melancholy. Where are the people? Spirits they may be, but truly, is not the land of the dead populated by those familiar from life; the flower-sellers, bread-makers, brewers, costermongers, farmers hawking their wares, tax-collectors, kingsmen, scribes, doctors, bone-setters and midwives? The people! The ordinary people, now dead, where are they?

The streets, even of death-town, ought be thronging with life after life. But no, all she could see were line after line of deserted streets, swept only by the wind. An old story floods into her mind, of Odysseus, communing with the dismal spirits of his departed friends, locked in the caverns of the night, ignorant of the correct formulae to pass on to the Elysium fields. Even Achilles, the hero, rooted there, obsessed with rebirth as the lowliest worm, anything rather than this living hell, even as most illustrious of the dead.

This cannot be right, cannot be right. Perhaps, she thought, they are sleeping, still in their tombs. She would go there, into the entranceways, which, though choked with rubble, offered only token resistance.

Zenobia shouldered her way into an undisturbed chamber. The picture is the same, are empty, all empty.

Then a stab of horror – no not true, she thinks, pushing the thought away, almost as quickly as it has arisen, have I stumbled into the tomb of a murderer! The clues are everywhere, the skeleton lying in disarray, and the neck glaring at her, fetish-like, nothing more than a skull on a pedicle. The body contracted, as if still in its death agony, the knees drawn up, fixed. This body was never once in the repose of Osiris, lying, as we all should, flatly on our backs, the arms crossed at the chest, nestling the soul.

The assemblage, if it happened at all, rushed and botched, where the head should be, just the remains of an ostrich shell – what an abomination. Sand everywhere, and red pots, that had once contained letters to the dead, now broken, the message so faint, she can barely know it at all. And in all this chaos, something is missing. Something has been taken at the hideous funeral feast. A tiny thing, a bone or the like. Everything here is anathema, the reverse image of how Osiris, Lord of westerners, should lead us in death.

But yes, she remembers, these people, they are after all those of Seth. To them what is black is white, what is green is red - everything is reversed – or – the thought again pops unbid into her mind – no surely it could not be, is it that Osiris is the parody?

The owner of this grave is long gone. How long, she wonders? Was there ever a time before? A strange thought possesses her, a technique from her previous life. She searches through the pile for one bone, a unique bone, the bone, that is, of memory. She huddles over it for an instant, just a moment, enough for her tongue to flicker over it. Memories pass from the flesh into her, as the saying goes, you are what you eat.

Her imagination is again flying, as visions force their way through, so with innocent eyes, she can again see all this as it once was. She can almost hear the trumpets of the funeral procession, as the relatives enter the boat-like tomb, freshly prepared by the experts, the body secretly dismembered, the head standing at the place of honour, as all that remember, weep, but also share of the feast, the special food, brought so far and at such expense. What is left, stuffed into special pots, whose red and black reminds Zenobia of a common curse, no not a curse, a blessing, then one tiny last piece of food, passed gingerly from hand to hand, for them to lick. Memory is all really, that and the return of the parts to the tribe, to live amongst those to come.

Her vision shifts, and for the first time Zenobia notices the frieze that adorns the entire curving wall of the womb like tomb. Its vivid colours, blood red and acidic yellow, dance in the heka light. The images are reflected and picked out on the pots, that lie in disarray in every direction – dozens of them. Images of the reed ferryboats, fashioned into the likeness of some huge aquatic beast, whose body carries them over.

What creature might that be? Seth again perhaps, who as Nemty ferries the souls across the river, yes, it could be him?

Like a feather dropping, Zenobia remembers, remembers how Seth's backbone, becomes the keel of a great ship, bearing up the body of his murdered brother. The yellow ochre and reds of the painting swim before her eyes –

celebrants dance around a circle at some final feast, presided over by the desert gazelle. Some are watching, their faces quiet, stoical, maybe sad? On the deck of the reed boats, a cabin of woven canes; at each of four quarters stands the wand of Seth. On the foredeck, a corpse – un-extended, crouched like a foetus awaiting the ferryboat to rebirth.

Silently witness to all these strange funeral rites, Zenobia suddenly feels that she too is being watched. The skin on the back of her neck is burning. Perhaps the spirits of the dead are here after all, and this place is not empty. Have they returned to the 'oh so many' empty tombs, the fields that should be alive with vast flocks of Ba birds, that until then have been far away and solitary?

With an enormous effort of will she forces herself to stare even more intently at the tomb freeze, fearing that any sudden curiosity on her part, will send these timid spirits back into the crannies of their hiding. Sweat gathers and falls down her back. There are faint shadows, just in the periphery of her vision, keeping pace with her, so that as her head moves ever so slightly, so too do the shadows move.

Zenobia's eye is again drawn to the worried faces of the celebrants, at the ancient funeral feast. Can they see something she cannot? After several minutes of this cat and mouse game, she can bear it no longer. On a reflex, she wheels around, expecting to see one or more of the spirits of the dead.

But nothing. Just the eerie feeling, the empty corridor receding into the gloom, a tiny dot of light at its far end. A wave of horripilation passes over her skin. She has an overwhelming desire to flee. The corridor is the only point of egress. She must go out the way she came in. She flies, lungs bursting, as she breaks out into the above ground. There to be greeted but only by the silent streets, in the city of the dead, bathed in a cadaverous light. But there, yes there again, yards away a tiny movement, as if someone turns into a side alley, again just out of sight. She must know, she must know.

Zenobia rushes to the alleyway, the first few yards choked full of fallen masonry. Thereafter it clears, she is running on, unimpeded for several hundred yards, back towards the ruined temple of Seth.

Before the temple, is the four square tower, that she instantly remembers as something that has appeared to her many times in dreams. On each cardinal is a regular door. This is the House of Life, the shade of a once magnificent scriptorium, attached to the temple, the prototype of all such buildings. It mimics the form of the first creation. In the days of the second coming stood such a scriptorium. Before then, the remnants of the first creation lay broken beneath the waters. The legend says seven sages come down from the stars to use the power of sound, to raise up the building. Four primeval gods took their foursquare stations. This is the seed point, the place of knowing. The reason the temple grew in this place. The words of the first gathering, imprinted on her mortal mind many years before, when as a child, Zenobia first entered the house of life as a priestess:

> 'Before me in the East Nephthys
> Behind me in the West Isis
> On my right hand in the South is Seth
> And on my left hand in the North is Horus
> For above me shines the body of Nuit
> And below me extends the ground of Geb
> And in the centre abideth the 'Great Hidden God.'

Her own quivering voice begins the liturgy; somehow she just knows, that before she reaches the end, another voice, will be compelled to blend itself with her own.

She finishes the liturgy with a question: 'who are you?'

20 The Bull of Ombos

> For I am knowledge and ignorance.
> I am shame and boldness.
> I am shameless; I am ashamed.
> I am strength and I am fear.
> I am war and peace.
> Give heed to me.
> I am the one who is disgraced and the great one.
> *The Thunder Perfect Mind*

Jay replied: 'I don't really know who I am. I've been lost and wandering in this place for days.'

'You?' Zenobia replied, without really knowing why. The disembodied part of her, was now nervous of its new companion. She felt this way, despite the fact she had just, breathlessly, tracked her halfway across the city.

Of course, part of her had been expecting to be among a vast crowd of the spirits of the dead. Instead she had found the necropolis eerily deserted. Now, finally, she had come across a companion among those spirits. But her interlocutor's confusion unnerved her, although it certainly confirmed their shared predicament.

Her new companion, though eccentric of dress, had an open, pretty face. It was as if Zenobia could gaze directly into her soul, the beating heart, buried deep in her breast, but looking all pink and pure. She felt a penetrating gaze gripping her own heart. The tension eased.

Zenobia's anxiety turned to compassion. They could be sisters. She must help end the confusion, help her to remember. She knew the trick of how a psyche, always paradoxical, had a tendency to hide itself from itself; of how the unreal could sometimes veil the real. Zenobia also knew how a mirror of reality could be broken by reality itself.

She took a deep breath then asked 'When you close your eyes what do you see?'

Jay fell silent for a moment then replied:

'I see a woman, she looks like me, only she's deathly pale. She must have been sick for quite a long time. Yes, the bed says it all, she's in a hospital. That will be it'

'Hospitalis?' Zenobia repeated the word, in a questioning manner, 'a guest house?'

'Ah yes,' her companion said, the penny dropping, 'sorry, my mistake, I meant klinikos.'

Zenobia understood. She pressed her, 'Wait,' she said, 'this woman in the klinikos, do you know her name? Take time to recall one.'

'Yes – her name is Jay, short for Jacky. Do you think that's me, that is my name?'

Zenobia nodded, 'Go on' she said, 'quickly, say more.'

'And may I have your name?'

'Yes of course, I am Zenobia.'

'Really?'

'And that is a familiar name to you?'

'Why yes, …'

Zenobia cut her short, suspecting this would be a digression. 'Do not bother yourself over that now; concentrate on the other things, you were telling me about the woman, Jay, on her bed, in the klinikos.'

'Well,' Jay continued, 'if that is me, I've been very sick. I remember travelling to Cairo, Memphis that is,' she quickly corrected. 'I was in the hospital for blood tests; the things the doctors did made it all worse. That's it, next thing I know I'm in this place. Only there's more to it than that – lots of hallucinations – like you now – you are one aren't you, a hallucination that is?'

'It is best not to worry about those things. Just tell me, do you know this place?'

'Not sure, a hallucination I suppose, opps sorry. OK it looks mightily like ancient Ombos, is it?

'I cannot really be sure,' Zenobia replied, 'but you know, my story and your story, they are similar. I cannot be sure what is true, what is my delirium. I was, I am sick, perhaps dying. I was brought to this place, now a crisis is coming, something will happen.'

'This place,' Jay interrupted, 'is a place of the head?'

'Yes.' Zenonia agreed, 'I have seen the truth of that. People lost their head in this place.'

'Something is going to happen to your broken head, my broken head.'

Zenobia shrugged. Then remembering her other self, waiting in the chapel, all in the hope that a doctor would appear to cure her clotted brain.

'I must go soon,' she said, 'at dawn, in a few hours, I must go before that.'

'Don't go', Jay pleaded, 'I've been so alone here. Let me come with you?'

'I will come back. There is business, here in the temple, but first I,' then seeing Jay's bleak stare, she corrected herself, '*we*, we must return to the encampment. I must check on my companions. Do you understand?'

Jay laid her hand on Zenobia's forearm. Zenobia felt the cool touch of the elegant, slender fingers:

'There is one thing.'

'Yes?'

'I think there is another, in there,' Jay flicked her head to emphasis *in there*, then continued: 'and I was thinking it must be you, but somehow, I've a feeling it must be someone else.'

'Show me.'

Jay led her to the ruined pylon at the eastern end of the temple. The roots of trees had invaded the stonework, causing the heavy lintels to collapse.

'Not here,' she said, 'come around to the northern wall, there's a doorway.'

Sure enough, a doorway of human scale, opened into the massive stone walls. Jay led her through a corridor threading its way inside the walls. They were just a few steps from the door, but already the darkness was crowding in on them. Zenobia glancing back toward the comforting oblong of light, some yards back the way they had come. Chiaroscuro, the blackness peppered by light shafting down from overhead apertures. The eerie effect as they saw one another's face, sometimes picked out by one of the overhead beams of light.

'How far is it?' Zenobia asked nervously

Jay could feel the anxiety in the question. The temple may be ruined, but different rules applied there.

'Not too far now', she answered with a little hesitation, 'I've not managed to get much beyond this point, but from the end of this long gallery, you can hear it quite clearly.'

'Hear what?'

'You'll see.'

They came, after maybe a hundred feet, to a point where the corridor veered off sharply to the left into another long gallery, that undoubtedly ran the entire width of the temple. This might well be the first portico, beyond which would be a pillared hall.

Jay gestured for Zenobia to be silent. They listened intently.

At first, just the very faintest of sounds, someone moving in the darkness, a low sigh, followed by a short series of gasps.

* * *

'What!' Jeuy shouted, startled, his voice laden with irritation. 'Oh it's you. And who's looking after Zenobia? Juey has been watching the familiar decans of stars marching across the heavens into the west. Throughout the passing hours of the night, the handle of the great adze, the opener of the mouth, clawed an arc of a great circle in the sky. Jeuy's eyes had grown heavy from squinting into the gloomy, moonlit horizon, hoping for the signs of an approaching caravan, with the promise of help from wise hands. But nobody came. Apart, that is, from Eko.

'It's OK,' Eko shouted back, at the same time thinking,

to himself, how ashen faced Jeuy now looked. He quickly told him how Sethnakht said he would stay with her for a while, just long enough for Eko to come see him, bring him some food. 'Should I go back now?'

Sethnakht was a boy not much older than Eko. A dark skinned goatherd, like his father before him, although lately drawn to the growing encampment of Beja warriors, to whom he sold his goat's milk cheese, or meat. Sethnakht had lingered too long with the men in their camps, listening to their tales of battle against the Romans. Now he too dreamt of proving himself with the iron spear, the bow, his knowledge of the desert.

'No, it's good,' Juey replied, his tension dissipating, glad to see Eko's friendly face, 'is there change?'

Eko did not reply, an answer of sorts. Juey knew the only hope was the physician coming in with the dawn. They sat together in silence, Juey munching some of the bread and goat's cheese. He was guiltily hungry still. Eko's young eyes scanned the horizon, while Jeuy ate.

'There,' he said suddenly, making Jeuy choke!

Juey dropped the clay bowl and jumped to his feet?

'What?'

'People are coming.'

Jeuy wasn't quite ready to believe his waiting was over.

Eko's eyes might be wrong. But then he saw it too, people were coming.

The long night vigil was over

* * *

Back in the temple, Zenobia's flesh was beginning to creep. She understood; she understood why Jay, her new companion Jay, otherwise a rational enough soul, had not managed to penetrate much further than their current vantage point.

The sighs grew louder, melding together until they became the familiar cries of a woman's bitter weeping, punctuated by a low, unintelligible muttering. There was no doubt that whoever or whatever was ahead in the darkness, they were admonishing themselves for their bitter fate.

* * *

Nearby, in the desert, a small party of Nubians was making its way down the scree at the base of the escarpment. Juey just knew the tallest of them must be Maimonides, the long awaited Ursennu. The aura of the traveller was so remarkable. The face of the elegant Nubian was refined, his lips full, his greying hair close cropped. Despite the physician's long night walk; he listened sympathetically to the details of

Zenobia's case. In a foreign though refined accent, his only request was to be given time to rest and prepare. Seeing the imploring looks on Eko's youthful face, Jeuy's hunched shoulders, he offered a final, reassuring promise, to do what he could. The delay, so he said, would be well used by his assistants, to make those preparations.

Zenobia's unnaturally motionless body lay within the cooling chapel walls. Her invisible Soulba fluttering nearby, drawn by the increased activity. Two sennu busied themselves in the cleaning, first the theatre of operations, then the patient, gently stripping her of her clothes, sponging her body with cool water infused with the unmistakable smell of Phoenician juniper. The sennu's powerful long fingers deftly removed the accumulated grime, the dried blood. The strong cedar smell reminded Juey of death. It seemed to Jeuy like they were fixing to embalm his friend. They continued to sponge her hair, drawing it back from her face. Her entire body was then swathed in clean linen.

When done, one of them gently lifted Zenobia up, cradling her head, doing his best to persuade tiny sips of a watery draft into her mouth.

Meantime, the other kindled fresh charcoal in a clay bowl. Soon it glowed red-hot, ready to receive a fistful of incense. A great column of natron rose into the air, curling up the walls, as the sennu quickly censed the room, leaving the still smoking dish at the foot of Zenobia's couch. When all was done, they made to depart, leaving final instructions for Eko and Juey not to feed their mamma. They too should wash thoroughly, body and clothes, take some food. Everyone was going to need strength.

Man and boy left Zenobia dozing peacefully and did as the sennu had ordered. They washed their bodies and changed into their best clothes. There was food for them to eat. They returned to the sick-room to renew their vigil over the deserted body of Zenobia. They meditated silently, sometimes they dozed beside her.

Before the sixth hour of the day, the midcourse of the sun, Maimonides swept silently into the room, making a beeline to his patient. He brought with him the strong smell of juniper oil, mixed with the renewed clouds of natron.

Crouching beside her, Maimonides read her vital signs, feeling the vessels in her neck, touching her skin, listening to her breathing, peeling back her eyelids to examine her pupils. He was ready to look at her most obvious wound. He removed the lint cover and passed the palm of his hand over it to sense the rising heat. He smelt it, prodded it, first with a finger, then with an elongated thumbnail.

In one effortless movement he rose again to his feet. He slid across the room to where Jeuy and Eko waited a respectful distance. In an instant he was at their side. He spoke in his quiet authoritative voice, assistants repositioned Zenobia's cot, letting a glaring shaft of sunlight fall upon her head.

His voice again.

'What I am about to do is not without risk. She may die now within a few minutes. Or she may live. But it is, in our opinion, her only chance. But you must say, shall I go on?'

Juey was speechless with grief. The blood had drained from Eko's young face but his voice was unwavering as he gave Maimonides his order: 'Just do it, please!'

The doctor, smiling grimly, let his gaze wander from Eko's face to Jeuy, then back to Eko. Just enough to register the adult's tiniest nod of agreement.

Maimonides suggested they wait outside, he would send word. Man and boy rose to leave, passing at the doorway others as they came in, one carrying a board covered in freshly washed instruments.

Zenobia's Soulba watched passively from her high vantage point as Maimonides intoned the physician's prayer:

Open to me, O heaven,
Open to me, O Earth
Open to me, O Underworld!

Open to me! I am Horus
I went forth from the necropolis of Wennefer.
May Imhotep Greatest of all physicians,
the son of Ptah,
Born of Kherti-ankh, guide me today!
May he tell me the prescription fitting to the illness,
Which has happened to our sister Zenobia,
Together with the skill to apply it,
And whether there be ignorance therein,
If so bear witness, bear witness!

O Imhotep the great, the son of Ptah,
Born of Kherti-ankh
Put the boat of reed on yourself
Place the bark of aru-wood under you,
While the heart of Ptah is on you.
It is as it should be
May he Imhotep the Great, son of Ptah born of
Kherti-ankh, be implacable against the illness in the
presence of Nephthys saying:
'O Shu, Live!
Oh soul life!
Live, O Shu, Live!
Live O Osiris,
Live, O Ethiopian soul!
Live, O Sokar who endures
Live, O great image of Egypt who rests in Memphis
Live, O Thoth and his father!
Come to our aid now
With the prescription which is fitting to the illness,

Together with the method for its application
That Zenobia, may Live!'

The words echoed around the chamber decaying to silence. Maimonides crouched beside his patient, again taking a long hard look at the wound, before seizing an exquisite blade of sharpened flint. His strong fingers gripped the tool. Deftly he made several short incisions, cutting through the fresh scar tissue to the bone. Zenobia's blood began to flow. He tore back a triangular flap of skin, the separation of each flap, accompanied by a distinct splitting sound as it came away from the bone. He called instructions to an assistant, for him to place his fingers to stop the flap of skin falling back into the wound. In this way he worked, exposing a neat, regular heptagon of raw flesh, at the front of Zenobia's bony skull.

The exposed bone, bruised by the missile, glistened in the strong beam of sunlight. Zenobia, invisible, studied Maimonides' face, close up, all the while he peered intently at the wound. Perspiration already peppering his intelligent brow. He looked up, making a low grunt, just enough for the assistant to proffer a strange instrument. To Zenobia this drill looked alarmingly brutal. Maimonides weighed it in his left hand, fitting the sharp end directly on the exposed bone.

Then, with the heal of his free right hand, he deftly struck the blunt end, driving it hard, penetrating the bone.

The drilling was accompanied by a crunching, grinding of bone and tissue. Zenobia's Soulba, safe in its cranny, had been watching with morbid fascination. But this shock wave set the bird-spirit flapping madly, panicking as it fell, dislodged from its perch. It was a real hammer blow to her own thin forehead. Balance lost, her invisible spirit fluttered unseen, rolling around the room, all the while, screeching in alarm.

* * *

'Aeeeeeeeeee!'

'What! What is it?'

She was back in the ruined temple, human again. Jay, her new companion was gripping her shoulders hard, shaking her?

Several moments had flowed over then in the pause, as they lingered before a dark corridor, unnerved by the pitiful sobbing, emanating from some dark space in a shrine before them. They had both been listening intently into the darkness just before Zenobia, without warning, burst out with this fearful screeching.

Zenobia came to her senses. Forcing herself to acknowledge she was again back in the deserted Temple of

Seth, contemplating whether to retreat, or move forward to investigate, and perhaps rescue a lost soul.

'I am calm, I am calm, stop shaking me, stop shaking me now!'

'Only if you're sure you're ok?'

'Yes,' she said, making an enormous effort to quieten her voice, to reassert control.

'I panicked that is all. It was something strange I saw. But I know what it was. I can bear it.'

Jay released her shoulders. She turned her head in the direction of the inner sanctum.

The sobbing had stopped. Whoever, or whatever was listening too, trying to fathom the source of yet another strange, confusing commotion, coming from a dark corridor.

'What did you see?' Jay hissed, 'Why did you shout like that?'

The look on Zenobia's face said she would rather not say. But Jay would have none of it.

'Go on, what did you see, tell me?'

'My friend, do you understand that we are not really in this space?'

'Yes,' she replied, all irony drained from her voice, 'It's some kind of delusion, hallucination, I know that.'

'It is more than that. That which we call the self, is divided into many parts, and for me and I think maybe for you, those parts have been forced apart and are lost or . . '

Jay finished the sentence for her,

'Or maybe we are dying and the parts are going their separate ways?'

A look of shock remained on Jay's face at the thought of what she had just said.

'Yes,' Zenobia spoke softy, 'it could be that.'

'So what did you see?'

Before replying Zenobia blew her nose on her sleeve.

'Somewhere, close by, in a klinikos, I saw my own body. There is something wrong, in here, in my head. I am clean and cared for. A great physician has come, to help me if he can. He will open my head.

I had a premonition of that — I see the gaping wound in my head, the bone beneath, the splintered skull, the brain of the skull broken open, the strong Nubian finger probing the skull. Something beneath, like wrinkles that form on poured metal, or hot wax as it cools. Then something inside, that trembles and flutters under those fingers, like the weak part of the top of a child's skull that has not yet become solid, how it pulsates. As the wound opens, something insides trembles and flutters like a wounded bird. Startled, I find myself scattering, back here again. Now do you understand?'

Pensively Jay replies 'Yes, I think I understand.'

There is a shocking, crashing sound behind them. Jay and Zenobia grab for each other, dumb with fear. Out of the darkness stumbles Madhavi, shouting, as she staggers into them both.

'Zenobia, Zenobia, is that your voice, please help me!!'

Jay is paralysed with terror. Zenobia, recovering her wits, although not quite her decorum, lets go her grip on Jay, instead seizing the once lovely body of her rival Madhavi. As she does so she hisses through clenched jaws:

'Courage, Madhavi! courage!'

The tension breaks. Soon all three women are sobbing, hugging each other amid calls of: 'I thought you would never come', mingle with 'peace, peace!', and 'what is to become of us!'

*　*　*

Maimonides is giving his final instructions. His assistant winds clean mummy cloth around Zenobia's broken head. Zenobia has survived. She is still unconscious. Maimonides, his shoulders beginning to sag with tiredness, leaves the room in order to tell Eko and Jeuy how things have gone. He is hopeful that she will soon wake. She must wake soon.

He tells how he has aspirated a very large blood-clot, that as he suspected, had built up beneath the bone. The skin flats had been closed over the aperture, but could be re-incised if he or his assistants sense that the clot was reforming. Otherwise the dressing would be kept in place. Zenobia is to be left to recover, with the hope, that soon the crisis would pass, and the brain would heal itself.

* * *

Back in the Temple. Zenobia squats close to Madhavi to talk. All are emotional, close to tears but she needs Madhavi to tell them about the song she had been singing in the god's sanctuary?

'Did you not recognise it, it was one I heard you recite long ago.'

'You have heard me sing?' Zenobia replies, her irritation again threatening to become obvious.

'Yes Zenobia, but I meant no harm. I was curious. I knew you were a chantress in the Temple of Isis. So I veiled myself to merge with the crowd. I was fascinated. Your voice is the best I heard there. Many lingered there just for the pleasure of listening. I was one of them.'

Zenobia sighed in recognition.

'Well,' she said, meaning to press Madhavi further, 'since

you are an admirer of my work, sing the song again, I must hear it. What was the song?'

Madhavi cleared her throat to utter the words:

'Beautiful youth, beautiful youth, come, come to your house . . .'

It was Jay who stopped her:

'That won't work here! Those are the lamentations of Isis and Nephthys. Lamentations are for Osiris.'

'Susssh,' Zenobia quickly interrupted, naively supposing the gods do not respond to whispers, 'do not speak so loud, do not mention his name here!'

So Jay went on in a whisper:

'Quite, this is the Mansion of Seth, the *murderer* of Osiris!'

Jay lingered over *murderer* as if spelling it out. Zenobia flinched. She stared directly into Madhavi's lotus like eyes. It was enough. Slowly the realisation dawned for Madhavi just why she was stuck, unable to make further progress through the temple. Her look of hope grew, maybe her strange new companions would bring an end to her ordeal. An end of some kind at least, perhaps Zenobia would also exact some revenge against Madhavi for stealing her husband's affections and bearing him a son.

'So what now?' Madhavi pleaded. It fell to Jay to reply, hardly able to resist a touch of irony.

'Good question.' she paused for effect. 'I recon we must all three advance to embrace fate. Prepare for an encounter with the one some say is the most violent and evil of all the Egyptian gods!'

'Zenobia, is that true!' Madhavi cried with some alarm.

'Yes, it is true!'

Zenobia meant to leave the rest unsaid. But seeing such a look of desperation on the beautifully naïve face of Madhavi, she was moved to reassure her.

'In your own country, do you not also have those beings, that are outwardly cruel and ferocious but keep a kinder, more benign face, for those that love them?'

Madhavi thought about this before replying. Then responded with words: 'Rudra-Shiva?'

It meant nothing to Zenobia who merely shrugged, leaving it for Jay to respond:

'Shiva! Yes, maybe like Shiva!'

Oh Murugan, she thought to herself, calling to mind an old friend and lover from a former life.

'Shiva,' Madhavi continued, repeating again the name of the strange Indian god. 'I understand that one. He is a great lover of women. And we are three women, beautiful in different ways. Zenobia, your red hair, your fast wits. I, the dark one, my mind only in my feet. Jay, she is funny, she is fair.'

Zenobia thought of her experiences back in the wadi, when the Roman had maimed and outraged her. In the darkest moments it was Seth who had come. Jay thought back to the dawn of time, before Osiris, before Isis, before Thoth, before Anubis, then only Seth, the ancient Bull of Ombos, the minotaur trapped in his labyrinth, searching for beloved Hathor or as it was then, the cow goddess, Bat, longing for her lord, Bata.

The three priestesses linked arms and advanced into the holy of holies with all the resolution they could muster. As they strode forward they chanted in unison, at first their voices weak and faltering then:

'Be not unaware of us oh Seth,
If you know us now, we shall know you!'

They struggled, past the blank mouths of the seven shrines, now apparently deserted and silent. They were drawn to the northern side of the crumbling temple where the light seemed to be stronger. Down a long corridor they went, past the cartouches of all the Egyptian kings since the beginning, and then, from a chamber ahead, they were hit by a wave of warm, rutty air.

In an enormous stone chamber they came to a circle of deliberately placed bucrania, at their centre, the packed red earth of a cattle pen. Strewn with fresh sand and straw, it was bathed in the wyrd red glow of hidden lamps.

The beast. He was there. The beast, dreaming of his lost herds in the desert pasturage. Circling and stamping, pawing the earth with his powerful foreleg. The great beast saw them. He eyed them with his steely glare. His withering look frightened them. But he was tethered to a bull stake, a ring of red carnelian passing through his nostrils.

Steam rose from his powerful chestnut pelt. Sweat streaked his back. His horns were massive and powerful. His hot breath condensed on them. His lips were damp, drooling with lust. On his forehead shone a single star. For Zenobia, Jay and Madhavi, it was a fixed point around which everything rotated.

Other hands join them. Their circle expanding, now they are seven. It was the ancient number of magick, the seven prophetesses of Hathor, the cow-goddess. They were the seven Hathors, who spin out a man's fate at birth. All of them were breathing together, lungs emptying and filling in time with the beast's audible drafts of air. Lines from a poem flow into Jay's mind.

> Turning and turning in the widening gyre,
> The falcon cannot hear the falconer
> Things fall apart
> The centre cannot hold . . .
> Mere anarchy is loosed upon the world.

Zenobia, Madhavi and Jay lay their hands on the flint mooring post, taking hold, fingers gripping the gold disk, the iron chain that holds the beast. It holds him there despite his hideous strength. Infected by its touch, they each see fate ravelling and unravelling, knowledge of all that has been, and is to be, flowing from the cool iron directly into their bodies.

Together, instinctively, they slide the ring of iron up towards the tip of the phallus-like pole. Into Zenobia's mind, come the words of an ancient spell:

'I remove the finger of Seth from the eye of Horus'.

Was it a womanly way that makes them stop as the ring nears the point of release. The women control it there, let it hang there, holding him back, allowing it to drop again.

The Minotaur's eyes redden with lust and desire. Its hot breath is on them. A second time they slide the ring up toward the tip, but again let it drop back to the root. It falls back with a earsplitting crash. Madhavi begins to chant lines in a strange tone, a tradition song of her homeland: 'namo Shivaya . . .

A third time they heave the tethering ring up to the tip. A little piece of them that is called Jay thinking to herself, *maybe this isn't such a good idea?*

Off it comes. With a grunt the hidden god is free. Hot starfire rains down on them. The Bull of Ombos stares for a moment, arches his neck, and leaps away from his prison. His earshattering bellows of triumph, cries of ochre victory, bounce like shock waves from the ancient stones. He is charging headlong through the enormous corridors. Still he bellows his triumph, joy uncontrollable, rushing, headlong through the streets of his city. Free at last, after centuries of stony sleep, free at last!

* * *

Jay awoke that day in her Cairo hospital bed. The drugs gone from her body. The place is deserted. Not a doctor or nurse to be seen. She presses her call button. Minutes tick by still no-one comes. *Oh well*, She says to herself, *nothing else for it but to sort myself out*.

Still unsteady on her legs, Jay struggles as far as the

deserted nurse's station. Nobody, just a transistor radio tuned to an Arabic channel. She catches the name of Egypt's pharaonic style president Sadat. After a guilty glance over her shoulder, Jay retunes to the BBC World service for the top of the hour news headlines. 'This is the BBC world service - the headlines - Egypt's president Anwar Sadat has been assassinated during a review of his country's armed forces.' The acting president Hussney Muburrak has declared a state of emergency.'

So what was all that? Just a dream. Somehow it seems more. Jay is sure that in another universe, in another place, Zenobia exists, staring into a horned mirror of bronze, admiring the new decoration to her familiar face, a seven pointed scar in the centre of her forehead. And when Zenobia closes her eyes, the vision somehow continues through this mark. She can still see the Bull of Ombos, the minotaur, waiting for her on the cliffs, tempting her to follow him, into the south, beyond Egypt, into his ancestral lands, into the land of Kush. Zenobia's adventure is about to begin again. And of one thing Jay is clear, she needs to find a less traumatic way of being a part of it.

Madhavi is more dead than alive. The smell of cardamom

is in her nostrils. The smell is not of death but of home! With agonising slowness she is emerging from the preternatural sleep brought on by the drugs fed to her by the followers of the holy man she had met in the Alexandrian forum. As a corpse she has been transported back to the land of her birth. As her senses quicken, the sounds of the ship creak their way into her consciousness. Though still hardly able to move she senses the passing days of her voyage across the ocean that divides her adopted Egypt from mother India.

Her strength is returning and with it the pain of a broken heart. She aches for her dead lover and for her lost child. Madhavi recalls the strange dreams that assailed her. She smiles at her own perversity, in that she now takes comfort from such evil sleep. Madhavi clings to the hope that Eko is safely in the strong, wise hands of one who also loves him. Her son's path is now entwined with that of strangers. He must wind his way into strange hidden lands. It will be a long journey before his day is done.

One day flows into another until Madhavi stands blinking in disbelief at the sight of a classical Roman temple, nestling among the tropical green of the coast hugging forest. Someone tells her it is a temple to the emperor, built beyond Rome's eastern frontier, for the colony of merchants and their garrison. Its has not yet been assimiliated by Mother India.

Madhavi has a premonition of how one day its alien lineaments will be rededicated to the goddess Isis. 'Here I shall wait for my son', she whispers to herself, hoping that Eko will one day come to find her and that this alien temple, so close to the port, would be the starting point for his search.

Glossary

Amon-Ra: see Ra

Anubis: A jackal-headed god who presided over mummification and accompanied the dead to the hereafter.

Apep, Apophis, demon of non-being, the opponent of Ra

'Ba' = 'soul' – after death, the person lives on in this form not on earth but in the tomb and the community's memory. Ba is the characteristic manifestation of a entiry, divine or human.

Barque of the Millions of Years: Ra's Manjet boat, with which he sailed through the 12 provinces of day. For his night journeys, Ra used his Mesket boat.

Bull of Meroe: Amon-Ra

Cartouche: A loop of cord with a knot at its base, in which the Pharaoh's name was written. The cartouche, the symbol of the Sun God's universal power - was thus reserved for use by the king .

Fortress for millions of years: On Thebes' west bank, the King's of the 18th, 19th and 20th Dynasties had large religious monuments built, which were improperly called 'funerary temples'. They were used to worship the deified pharaoh.

Cheth = CTh or Seth. A vox magica - ie hidden name granting power

Dendara: The capital of the sixth Nome of Upper Egypt. Its necropolis contains tombs dug between the Predynastic period and the end of the Old Kingdom. This site's renown is due to the famous Temple of Hathor, which dates back to the Greco-Roman period. Dendara was dedicated to Hathor, one of the oldest Egyptian deities, represented as a cow or a woman with cow's ears.

Djed: A pillar, symbol of stability and duration; it represents Osiris' spinal column. It is also a protective amulet.

Decanal: 36 'stars' on the belt of the southern ecliptic, whose rising was used to mark the passage of the 'hours' during each cycle or 'week' of ten days.

Egyptian: A language of the Hamiti-Semitic group which includes Semitic, Berber, Cushitic and Hausa.

Ennead: A group of more or less nine deities, such as the Ennead of *Heliopolis* - Atum, Shu and Tefnut, Geb and Nut, Osiris and Isis, Seth, Nephthys.

Harpoon: The main weapons used for hunting hippos.

Hathor: This cow-headed deity (sometimes depicted as a woman with cow's ears) protected women and the dead, as she was likened to the Goddess of the Kingdom of the Dead; she was also goddess of music and intoxication.

Horus: God of the sky and protector of the pharaoh who was likened to him. Horus could be depicted as a falcon-headed man. As the son of Osiris and Isis, he was often represented as an infant (Harpocrates) with a finger held to his lips.

Intercalary: Twelve lunar months of 30 days equals 360, which leaves five extra or intercalary days, on which the priests of Heliopolis assigned the birth of five gods, almost as a supplement to their own theological system. The five gods said to be born on these days were: Osiris, Isis, Seth, Nephthys and Horus the child. This schema is known from Pyramid Text 1961 and Plutarch, *Isis and Osiris*.

Ladder of Seth: means by which the king's soul rises to the stars. Made of iron that has fallen from the heavens. Jacob's ladder may also be a meteorite.

Lettuce (Lactuca sativa) was considered an aphrodisiac in Egypt and Mesopotamia. Eaten by Min, god of fertility and Seth. Contain small amounts of an opiate later reduced by cultivation.

Meroe: Capital city of the kingdom of Kush (4th century BCE to 4th century CE).

Maat heru: Speaking true, which will get you through the gates after judgement (lxvi).

Maat: Divine personification of the cosmic order, secondarily connected to the concepts of truth and justice. She has no folklore and originates as a philosophical abstraction. She wears an ostrich plume headdress.

Min: One of the oldest and greatest of Egyptian gods. A storm deity, often shown with an erection. Probably an old indigenous god of Koptos & Panopolis. Equated by the Greeks with their god Pan.

Mut: The wife of Amon venerated in Thebes. Originally depicted as a vulture, she later took on a human form.

Naos: A small chapel of stone or wood inside the sanctuary in which the god's effigy was kept.

Neter: God or the Divine.

Nehes: Nubia; (later Kash: Kush), the derivation of 'Nubia' may be from 'Nub' - meaning gold.

Neith: Goddess of the hunt and war, cult centre at Sais.

Nome: One of forty-two administrative districts, significantly also the number of the judges of the dead. Interestingly each Nome coincides with one of the enormous temporary lakes caused by the annual Nile flood (Butzer 1976).

Osiris: The husband of Isis; after his murder by his brother, Seth, he fathered a son, Horus, who, grown to adulthood, avenged him. He is represented with his crown (atef), his scepter (bequa), and his flail, (nekhekh).

Pan: See Min

Pharaoh: Egyptian word for king is 'nsw' - 'pharaoh', as used in the Bible is probably derived from per'o - 'king's house'.

Ptah: The God of Memphis, where he was believed to have brought the universe into being; the husband of the Lion Goddess, Sekhmet, he was depicted wearing a mummy's shroud, holding in his hand a scepter. He was later likened to another Memphis god of death, Sokaris, and was worshipped in his syncretic form of Ptah-Sokaris.

Pylon: A monumental temple entrance, consisting of a portal between two enormous trapezoidal monoliths.

Ra, or Re, as Egyptian sun-god Ra, who was beholden to Seth for defending against the demons who assailed him on his daily journey through the skies.

Sekhmet: Lion-headed goddess, sometimes crowned with the solar disk. She protected the royal power; she can be likened to Hathor, Bastet and Isis.

Seth: One of the oldest & indigenous gods of Egypt. The origins of his cult are lost in mists of prehistoric time.

Complex and highly ambiguous diety, later seen as the passionate and violent emanation of the great solar creator - Amun-Ra. Seth's cult widely demonised

Setna, Khamuas: Khaemwase, son of Ramesses II and Isis-Nefert. He died in the 55th year of the reign of his father. He was sem-priest of Ptah and chief artificer.

Sycamore, Lady of the Southern : epithet of Hathor at Memphis, where she assisted Horus after he had been blinded by Seth.

Thebes: During the 18th Dynasty (ca.1550 - 1295BC), the city of Weset was founded by Amenhotep I; better known by its Greek name, Thebes, it became the heart of the country. It was at this time that the Great Temple of Amon in Karnak became the country's most important religious center and the royal necropolises were excavated in the Valley of the Kings and the Valley of the Queens.

Ursa Major: The Great Bear, The Plough, Meshketyu. Constellation associated with Seth.

Ursa Minor - 'Small Bear' another significant northern constellation, the location of the current pole star *Polaris*, the target of Seth's constellation *Ursa Major*.

Wadj: A scepter in the form of a papyrus stalk, it was characteristic of female deities.

PAN'S ROAD

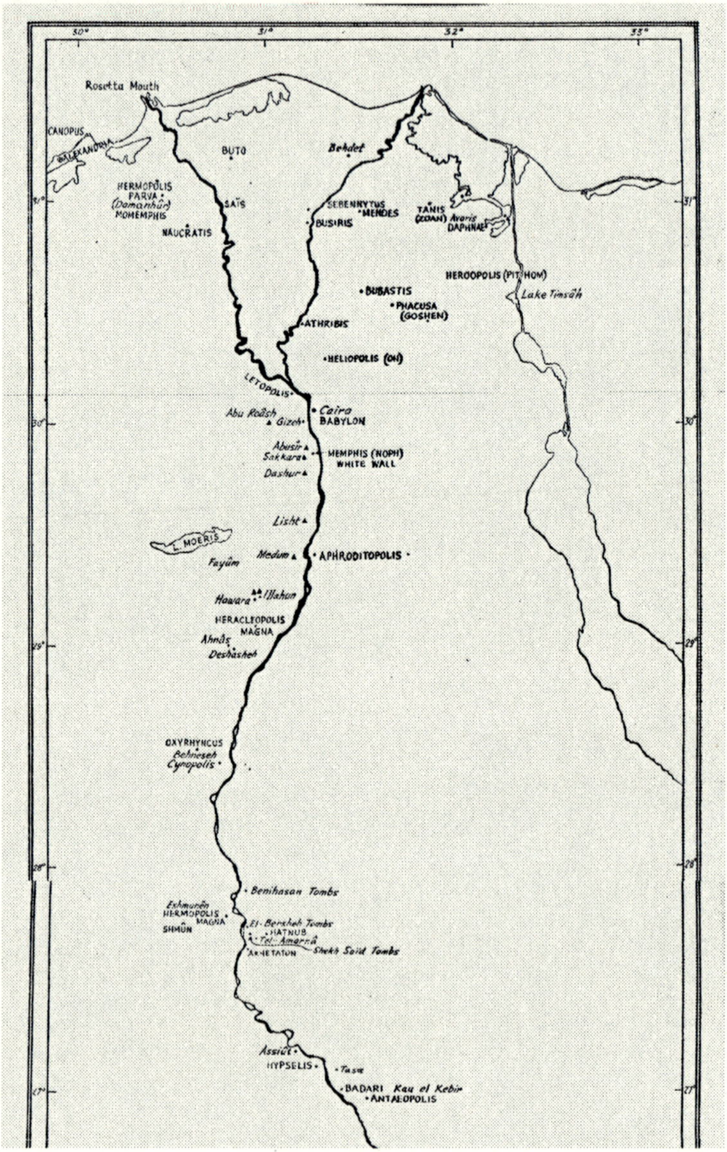
30°
31°
32°
33°
Rosetta Mouth
CANOPUS
ALEXANDRIA
BUTO
Behdet
HERMOPOLIS PARVA
(Damanhûr)
MOMEMPHIS
SAÏS
NAUCRATIS
SEBENNYTUS
MENDES
BUSIRIS
TANIS (ZOAN)
Avaris
DAPHNAE
HEROOPOLIS (PITHOM)
Lake Timsâh
BUBASTIS
PHACUSA (GOSHEN)
ATHRIBIS
HELIOPOLIS (ON)
LETOPOLIS
Cairo
BABYLON
Abu Roâsh
Gizeh
Abusir
Sakkara
MEMPHIS (NOPH)
WHITE WALL
Dashur
Lisht
L. MOERIS
Fayûm
Medum
APHRODITOPOLIS
Hawara
Illahun
HERACLEOPOLIS MAGNA
Ahnâs
Deshâsheh
OXYRHYNCUS
Behneseh
Cynopolis
Benihasan Tombs
Eshmunên
HERMOPOLIS MAGNA
SHMÛN
El-Bersheh Tombs
HATNUB
Tel-Amarna
AKHETATON
Shekh Saïd Tombs
Assiût
HYPSELIS
Tasa
BADARI
Kau el Kebir
ANTAEOPOLIS

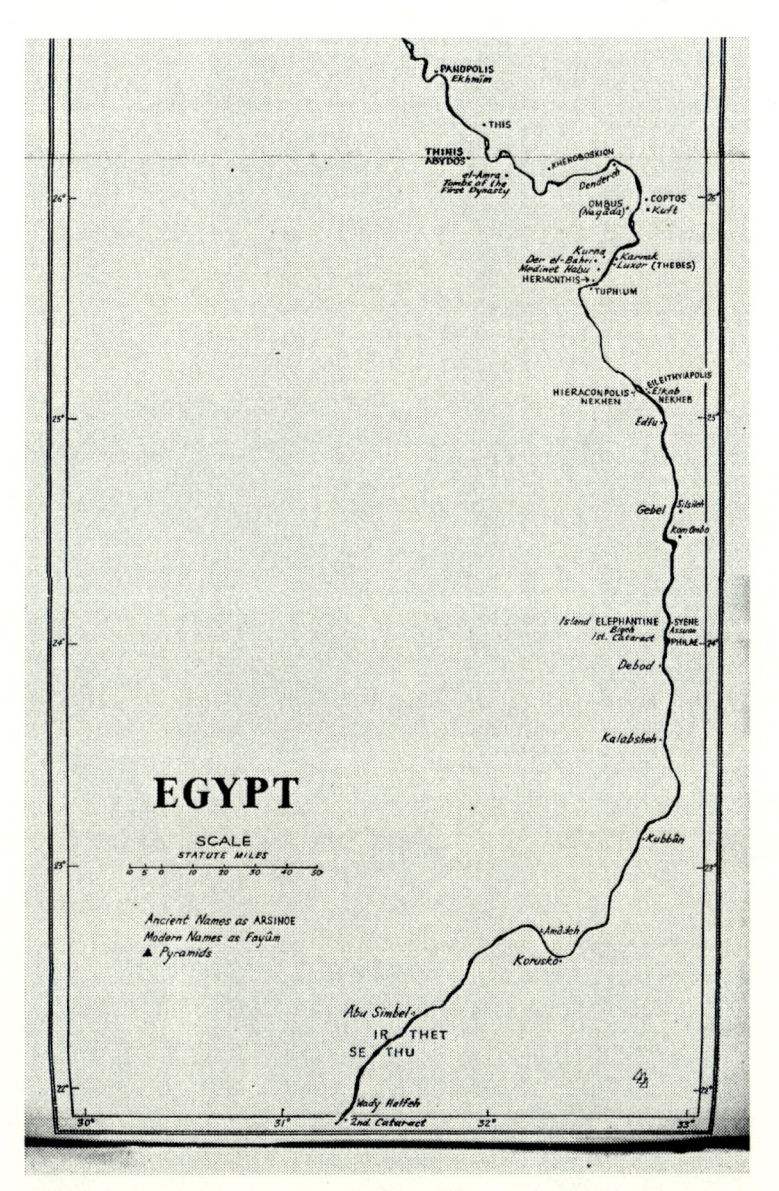

PAN'S ROAD

EGYPT

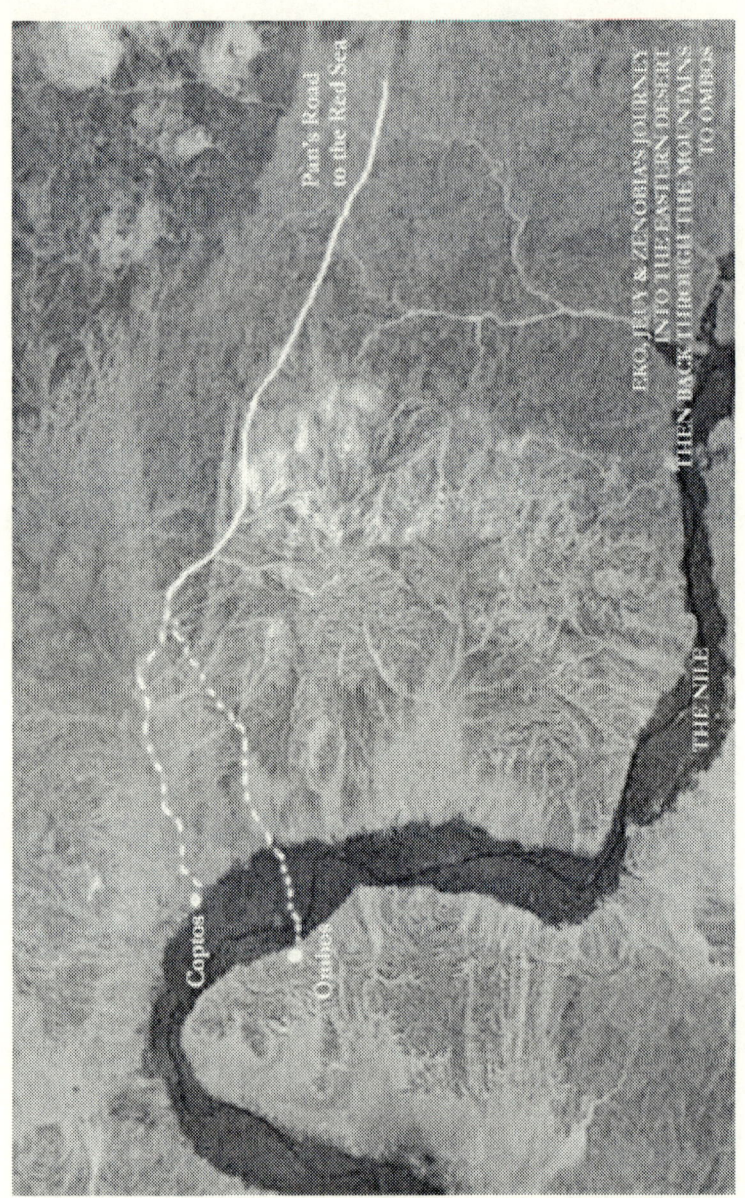

Based on a 'Google Earth' image

231

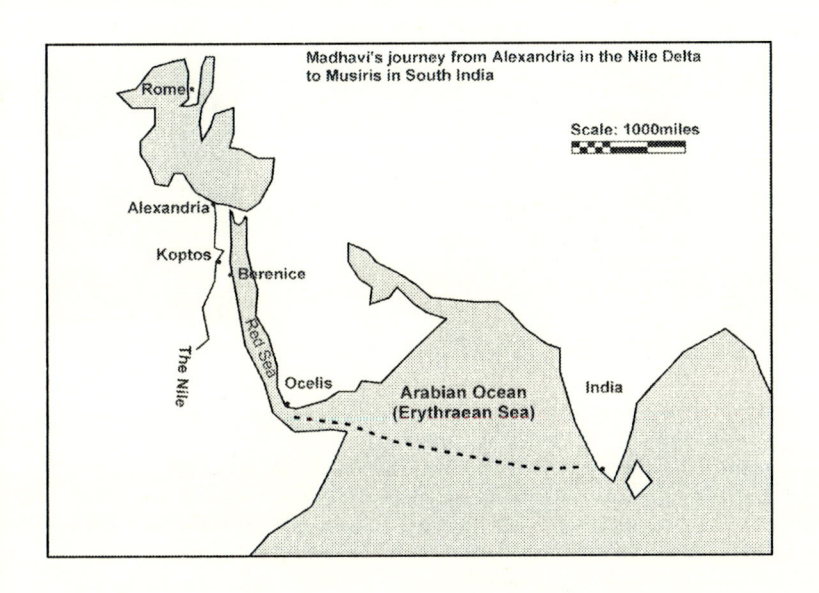

Mandrake

A Related Title
The Bull of Ombos
Seth and Egyptian Magick II
Mogg Morgan

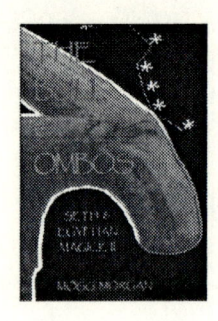

Naqada is a sleepy little town in Upper Egypt, that gives its name to a crucial period in the prehistory of Egypt. In 1895, William Matthew Flinders Petrie, the 'father' of Egyptian archaeology, stumbled upon a necropolis, belonging to a very ancient city of several thousand inhabitants. With Petrie's usual luck, he'd made yet another archaeological find of seismic proportions – not just an ancient city a quarter the size of Ur in Mesopotamia, a rare enough find, but the capital of the earliest state established in Egypt! Petrie's fateful walk through the desert led him to a lost city, known to the Greeks as Ombos, the Citadel of Seth. Seth, the Hidden God, once ruled in this ancient place before it was abandoned to the sands of the desert. All this forbidden knowledge was quickly reburied in academic libraries, where its stunning magical secrets had lain, largely unrevealed, for more than a century - until now.

Contents: Gold in the desert / Sethians and Osirians compared / Cannibalism /Temple of Seth / Seth's Town / Seth as Bull of Ombos / Hathor / The names of Seth / Animals of Seth / Seth - the red ochre god / Seth and Horus / Opening the mouth / Seven / The Boat / Heka & Hekau / Magical activities / Cakes of Light / Magick as use and misuse of the funeral rite / Re-emergence of the Hidden God / Five useful Appendices / Extended bibliography /Glossary /

For these & other titles contact:
Mogg Morgan, (01865) 243671
mandrake@mandrake.uk.net
web: mandrake.uk.net
PO Box 250, Oxford, OX1 1AP (UK)